The Witches of Friar's Lantern

By
Sandra Forrester

All inquiries should be addressed to:
Barron's Educational Series, Inc.
250 Wireless Boulevard
Hauppauge, New York 11788
http://www.barronseduc.com

Library of Congress Catalog Card No.: 200234274

International Standard Book No.: 0-7641-2436-6

Library of Congress Cataloging-in-Publication Data
Forrester, Sandra.
    The witches of Friar's Lantern / by Sandra Forrester.
        p. cm.
    Summary: Trying to undo the spell of the evil Dally Rumpe, Beatrice
travels to Werewolf Close, where she meets two of her mother's aunts and
learns something about her mother's past.
    ISBN 0-7641-2436-6
    [1. Witches—Fiction.] I. Title.

PZ7.F7717 Wi 2003
[Fic]—dc21

2002034274

PRINTED IN THE UNITED STATES OF AMERICA

9 8 7 6 5 4 3 2 1

Contents

The Maps of
Bailiwick

BAILIWICK

Skull House

Blood Mountain

Swamp

Swamp

Woods

Merriwether House

Muttering Lane

Cattail Court

Friar's Lantern

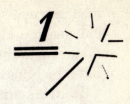

1

The Magic Touch

On this bright, cold Saturday in December, it seemed that everyone in town was stopping by the Bailey Nursery and Garden Center for evergreen wreaths and mistletoe. People might whisper about the Baileys among themselves, relishing the exchange of tidbits regarding the family's peculiar—and some even dared to suggest *witchlike*—behavior, but that didn't stop the gossips from flocking to the nursery. It was a well-known fact that Mr. and Mrs. Bailey had the magic touch when it came to plants.

Beatrice Bailey had been assigned the task of arranging a shipment of holiday lawn ornaments at the front of the store. But instead of snowmen and reindeer, Beatrice found herself staring at thirty-six of the ugliest garden gnome sprinklers she had ever seen. The gnomes were obviously a shipping error, but Mr. Bailey had said with his usual practicality, "It's too late to reorder. Just stick some candy canes in the holes on their heads and we'll call them Santa's helpers."

Beatrice was now surveying the results skeptically. They looked like an army of ill-tempered space aliens with striped antennae poking out of their foreheads. Beatrice could imagine kids all over town taking one look and announcing to their parents, "I don't *want* Santa to come. What if he brings his elves?"

Beatrice's friend, Teddy Berry, was perched on a nearby counter, thumbing through a fashion magazine and pointedly ignoring the commotion around her.

"So what do you think?" Beatrice asked Teddy.

Teddy looked up, blinked twice, and started to giggle.

It was the response Beatrice had expected.

"Beatrice, can you and Teddy give me a hand?" Mr. Bailey called out as he emerged from the storeroom with an armload of boxes. Overzealous customers jostled him as they grabbed for pots of poinsettias at his elbow, causing the boxes to teeter precariously.

Beatrice was only too happy to abandon her nightmarish elf creations. Then she saw the boxes in her father's arms, and frowned.

"Oh, no," Teddy said, expressing Beatrice's feelings exactly. "Is that what I think it is?"

"Strings of lights," Beatrice said in a resigned voice. "Many, *many* strings of lights."

"Your dad keeps adding to them every year," Teddy protested. "We'll be here all night putting them up, and I wanted to go to the mall. It *is* the first day of Winter Break!"

"You don't have to stay," Beatrice said, but she gave her friend an imploring look.

"I promised your dad I'd help while we're out of school," Teddy said grudgingly.

Beatrice raised her eyebrows, but kept her comments to herself. She *could* have said that drooling over winter fashions in *Traditional Witch* for the past two hours wasn't really helping. But Beatrice knew that Teddy meant well; she was just naturally self-absorbed. And at least she had been discreet enough to keep the magazine cover hidden from all the mortals milling around. Even so, Beatrice's parents would be appalled if they saw anything even remotely witchy in their nursery. Mr. and Mrs. Bailey believed in trying to fit in.

Beatrice and Teddy, who had been best friends since they were four, were twelve years old. Teddy was petite and strikingly pretty, with brown curly hair and dark eyes behind oversize wire-rim glasses. No one had ever called Beatrice pretty that she could remember, but she was happy enough with her looks when she gave them any thought at all. Tall and skinny was what she saw when she looked in the mirror. A closer inspection revealed pale red hair cut straight across at the shoulder, a fringe of silky bangs that habitually fell into her eyes, and an angular face that had a distinct feline quality about it. Even her large green-gold eyes resembled those of a cat.

Beatrice blew her bangs aside and said, "We'd better go help him."

"You *owe* me," Teddy informed her.

They squeezed through the crowd to where Mr. Bailey was happily unpacking one of the boxes. "Twelve strands here," he said cheerfully, not seeming to notice the girls' lack of enthusiasm. "Beatrice, can you plug these in and see if any bulbs are burned out? Teddy, just grab a box, any box."

At that moment, a large long-haired mop of a cat—predominantly black, with dashes of orange and white—sailed with surprising grace from the top of an eight-foot balsam fir and landed amid the pile of lights. Beatrice reached down to scoop up the cat, who then leaped to Beatrice's shoulder and promptly began to purr.

"Cayenne, why have you been hiding all day?" Beatrice asked as she scratched behind one of the big cat's ears.

"My guess is, she finds those Santa's helpers"—Teddy lowered her voice delicately—"a *lit-tle* scary."

"No scarier than the people buying them," Beatrice murmured, watching as gnome after gnome was plucked up with delight.

Twenty minutes later, Beatrice was shaking her head and muttering, "Fifty-eight strands of lights."

Mr. Bailey, who was tall and skinny like his daughter, stood up and stretched the kinks out of his long frame. "Yeah, isn't it great? There's enough to decorate inside and out!"

Mrs. Bailey was checking out a long line of customers nearby. "Hamish, do you have to do that now?" she called to her husband. "We need to open the other register."

"I will, Nina," Mr. Bailey assured her. "With the girls' help, we'll have this done in a jiff."

Mrs. Bailey just rolled her eyes.

Beaming at the bounty spread out at his feet, Mr. Bailey said, "I'll get the ladder and start hanging these from the rafters."

"We'll still be here this time tomorrow," Teddy grumbled.

Although Beatrice and Teddy had no way of knowing it, at that exact moment they were being watched. Two executives at the Witches' Institute were seated in front of what appeared to be a large computer screen, observing and listening to all the goings-on at the Bailey nursery. The thirty-something female witch was elegant and uncommonly attractive, with auburn hair spilling over the shoulders of her green silk robes. The man had a long, bloodhound kind of face, his expression solemn but genial, and a cap of thick brown hair that stood out around his head like a toadstool.

"I don't know about this electronic spying," the male witch said, his brows drawing together in a frown. "Do you think the new technology is entirely ethical, Aura?"

"It isn't *spying*, Leopold." Aura Featherstone had spoken more sharply than she intended, perhaps because of her own reservations about the recently installed Magi-monitors. "We have to observe young witches in order to classify them correctly, don't we? It was difficult enough to keep up with everyone inside the Witches' Sphere, but remember all those reconnaissance trips to the mortal world?"

"And having to masquerade in mortal clothing," Leopold Meadowmouse added, recalling with distaste when mortals were big on bell bottoms and polyester knits.

The flowing purple robes he was wearing now were far more comfortable—not to mention more *dignified*.

"When the Executive Committee voted on the monitors, there were eleven for and two against." Aura glanced shrewdly at her companion. "You were one of the two dissenters, weren't you, Leopold? Don't look so guilty," she admonished him with a hint of amusement in her voice. "I voted against them, as well." Then she sighed, and turned her attention back to the screen. "But there's no fighting progress, I suppose. And these monitors are a blessing in murky cases like Beatrice Bailey's."

"Bailiwick," Dr. Meadowmouse murmured absently, and bent closer to the screen, where he could see Beatrice stroking her cat-familiar and Teddy leaning against the counter with a bored expression on her face. "Don't you remember, Aura? Bailey was the name they took when some long-ago Bailiwick moved to the mortal world and went Reform."

"Of course. Beatrice *Bailiwick*," Dr. Featherstone corrected herself.

"Teddy Berry seems to be in a bad mood every time we tune in," Dr. Meadowmouse remarked.

"She's furious with us," Dr. Featherstone answered. "She thought we would have brought them back to the Witches' Sphere by now for the next part of their test. Not that I blame Teddy. I was just like that at her age—ready to set the world of magic on fire and impatient with anyone who stood in my way."

"Beatrice is handling the delay with more maturity," Dr. Meadowmouse observed. "But then, unlike Teddy, Beatrice doesn't care *how* we classify her."

6

"I don't know about that," Dr. Featherstone said. "Personally, I believe Beatrice would be thrilled with a Classical classification."

"She keeps saying otherwise." Dr. Meadowmouse rifled through a thick stack of papers in front of him. "'What does a dumb classification mean, anyhow?'" he read. "That's a direct quote, Aura. And then she told Teddy, 'All this aspiring to be a *great witch* takes the joy out of everything.' And she also said, 'I don't care if they *never* make me a Classical witch. I *like* being an Everyday witch.'"

Dr. Featherstone cast an indulgent glance at her colleague. "Of course she *says* that, Leopold. She's lived her whole life among mortals, and audacity isn't one of their strong suits. Don't you see? If we classify Beatrice Everyday, we're telling her that she isn't capable of important magic, that we don't expect anything more dazzling from her than conjuring up the occasional thunderstorm. She's just trying to shield herself from disappointment."

"When Beatrice turned twelve last October," Dr. Meadowmouse said thoughtfully, "the rest of the committee voted to classify her Everyday. You were the only one to suggest that we test her Maximum Magic Level."

"So?"

"So . . . we rarely test young witches. In fact, practically never. It's usually obvious by the age of twelve if a witch has exceptional talent."

"What are you trying to say, Leopold?" Dr. Featherstone was beginning to sound impatient.

"I'm *saying* that we didn't test Teddy Berry before we classified her Everyday—nor did we test those other two friends of Beatrice's. And frankly," Dr. Meadowmouse concluded, not unkindly, "I don't see that Beatrice has any more ability—magically speaking—than they do."

Aura Featherstone's eyes flashed dangerously as they bore into his face. "Then perhaps we gave Beatrice's friends the wrong classification," she said in a voice that was deceptively calm. "That's why I thought it only fair to reevaluate them when they volunteered to help her. And they did pass the first part of the test, didn't they? Brilliantly, I might add. I hardly think that getting past an enchanted hedge of thorns and defeating a fire-breathing dragon was just beginner's luck. Do you?"

"It might have been," Dr. Meadowmouse answered honestly. "Look, Aura, I'm as fond of Beatrice Bailiwick as you are. But I can't help wondering . . ."

"*What*, Leopold?"

"Why you've taken such an extreme interest in this young witch," he said bluntly. "From the beginning, you were determined to test her, and *The Bailiwick Family History* gave you a legitimate reason to do so. That's a thick book, Aura." Dr. Meadowmouse looked at her steadily. "I admire the tenacity that kept you at it until you found the one line that suited your purpose. As the eldest—actually, *only*—Bailiwick female in her generation, the responsibility falls on Beatrice to try to break the spell cast against her ancestors. You couldn't have designed a better test yourself."

"And the fact that she's done so well only proves my point," Dr. Featherstone said smugly. "Bailiwick witches have been trying to undo Dally Rumpe's spell for two hundred years, and they've all failed. *Until Beatrice*. And don't forget—you did support me in testing her."

"Haven't I *always* supported you?" He smiled at her with amusement and obvious affection.

"Yes, you have," she agreed, appearing somewhat placated.

"And I'll continue to do so," Dr. Meadowmouse said. "But I do have misgivings about this. We put those young witches into serious danger when we sent them on the first Noble Quest, as you called it. And there are still four parts of the test to go. I have concerns about placing them in harm's way again and again."

His words served to douse the fire in Dr. Featherstone's eyes. "So do I," she said quietly. "But whether we intervene or not, trying to break the curse against the Bailiwicks is Beatrice's destiny. Isn't it?" she asked, searching his face for confirmation or denial.

Dr. Meadowmouse hesitated, then nodded reluctantly. "It's written in *The Bailiwick Family History* that Beatrice must try to reverse the spell," he said. "But, Aura, she never would have read that history if we hadn't shown it to her."

Mr. Bailey had come back dragging a ladder. "Don't you love the smell of cedar?" he enthused. "All we need to make the day perfect is a good old-fashioned snowstorm."

Beatrice perked up. "I can handle that," she said, and turning away from the crowd, began to whisper:

Circle of magic, hear my plea,
Blowing winds,
Blinding snow,
These, I ask you, bring to me.

Beatrice had scarcely uttered the final word when customers started pointing out the windows and exclaiming, "It's snowing! Will you look at that? The weatherman predicted a sunny weekend!"

"Way to go," Teddy said, grinning at her friend. All it took was a little magic to brighten Teddy's outlook.

"*Now* the day is perfect," Mr. Bailey said. Although he generally didn't encourage his wife and daughter to use magic in public, Beatrice's ability to control the weather—*consistently and brilliantly*, he had once told Mrs. Bailey—never failed to make Mr. Bailey proud. It didn't bother him a bit that Beatrice had never been able to master any other kind of spell.

Beatrice and Teddy began draping lights at ground level, while Mr. Bailey hung them from the ceiling. A few minutes later, Teddy stood back with her hands on her hips to survey their progress.

"This is taking too long," she said. Then lowering her voice so that only Beatrice could hear, Teddy added, "I read a spell in *Modern Witch*—"

"*Teddy*." Beatrice gave her friend a warning look.

"I know," Teddy said airily, "there's only one spell I can cast with any degree of precision. But how am I ever going to improve if I don't practice?"

"Practice at home where you can mess up your own stuff," Beatrice said sternly, and looped a strand of lights around a display of pinecone wreaths. Cayenne extended a black-and-white paw from her nest among the wreaths and snagged the lights.

"Come on, Beatrice," Teddy pleaded. "Let me try. If it doesn't work—"

"You mean, if you should blow up the building instead?" Beatrice said pointedly. "I don't think my parents' insurance covers magical incompetence."

But the truth was, Beatrice was getting tired of stringing lights herself. "Besides, everyone would see you do it," she said, glancing nervously around the crowded nursery.

Teddy could tell that her friend was cracking. "They'll go up so fast, no one will even notice," she said eagerly.

"It's not a good idea to show off in front of mortals," Beatrice insisted. "Have you forgotten the Salem witch trials?"

But Teddy wasn't listening. She was already mumbling under her breath:

Lights be lively, lights be quick,
Dress this room lickety-split,
On the ceiling, around the door,
Strand by strand, from roof to floor.

"Teddy, don't—" Beatrice began, and then she yelped! A string of lights had whipped out of her hands and was dancing through the air.

Beatrice's mouth fell open in astonishment as all fifty-eight strands of lights seemed to come alive at once. They writhed across the floor and countertops like twinkling neon reptiles, coiling themselves around posts and table legs and—*Oh, no!* Beatrice thought hysterically—the ankles of startled customers.

Suddenly the room was filled with screams and the flailing of arms and legs as terrified people tried to escape the tenacious grip of the runaway lights. Then bulbs began to explode, causing windows to rattle and streams of red and blue and green fire to shoot skyward like fireworks.

Teddy stood frozen, an expression of horrified disbelief on her face. "What have I done?" she whispered.

That's when Beatrice noticed that a strand of lights had encircled the wreath where Cayenne was nestled, and was now squeezing the cat in a snakelike embrace.

With a startled cry, Cayenne sprang into the air and streaked up the nearest fir to its highest branches. The top of the tree swayed giddily under the cat's ample weight. Holding on for dear life with every claw, Cayenne shot Beatrice a look of fury.

"Counterspell!" Beatrice yelled to Teddy.

"*What!*" Teddy had to back against the wall to keep from being trampled by people running for the door.

"Is there a counterspell?" Beatrice shouted.

"Uh—yes." Teddy paced and flapped her hands frantically as she tried to remember. "It's something like—*Lights reverse, and I'll be happy*—"

"Yes?" Beatrice prodded when Teddy stopped.

"*Undo this spell*—uh—*undo this spell*—"

"We got that part," Beatrice said in exasperation. "*Undo this spell . . .*"

"*—and make it snappy,*" Teddy mumbled. "I think that's right."

"Or close enough," Beatrice said. "Look."

All around them strands of lights stopped whipping and coiling in midair, then fell in a lifeless heap to the floor.

Beatrice and Teddy had about three seconds to feel relieved. That was when they looked across the now deserted nursery and saw Beatrice's grim-faced parents coming toward them. But they were saved from whatever the Baileys meant to say to them by the appearance of something far worse.

The front door opened and Beatrice's heart sank when she saw Amanda Bugg peering inside, looking exactly like a weasel ready to pounce on an unsuspecting mouse. And as if it weren't bad enough having her least favorite classmate show up at the worst possible moment, Amanda had brought her nauseating friend, Olivia Klink, with her.

"Hi, Beatrice," Amanda said brightly, her sharp eyes taking in the signs of disarray left by fleeing customers and lights run amok. "No shoppers today? I would have thought this close to the holidays . . ." The girl's voice trailed off and she regarded Beatrice with a meaningful smirk.

Beatrice tried to keep from scowling at Amanda, and nearly succeeded. "Can I help you with something?" Beatrice asked curtly.

"Well . . ." Amanda looked around doubtfully. "Everything seems *picked over*, doesn't it, Olivia?"

"We didn't come to shop, anyway," Olivia blurted out, then cringed visibly as Amanda's stare impaled her.

What a surprise, Beatrice thought sourly. The only reason Amanda and her friends ever came near the Baileys was to pry into Beatrice's personal business. The girl seemed to have made it her life's mission to prove that something was not quite right with the Baileys.

"So are you enjoying Winter Break?" Amanda asked sweetly. "I thought you and Toady here would be hanging out with your boyfriends."

"That's *Teddy*," Beatrice said coldly.

"Ms. Berry to you," Teddy hissed through clenched teeth.

"And Ollie and Cyrus are *friends*, not boyfriends," Beatrice added, immediately wondering why she let this obnoxious mortal bait her.

Beatrice sighed, suddenly feeling very tired and wanting more than anything for Amanda to leave. "If we can't help you find something, you'll have to excuse us," she said abruptly. "We have a lot of work to do."

"I can *see* that," Amanda said with disdain. "Actually, we only stopped by to find out why everyone was running out of here screaming. Beatrice, I'll let you in on a little secret," she added, her voice suddenly dripping kindly concern. "Your public relations techniques aren't working."

With an especially nasty grin, Amanda flipped her hair over her shoulder and started for the door. A snickering Olivia Klink followed close on her leader's heels.

The only positive outcome of Amanda's visit was that Mr. and Mrs. Bailey's angry faces had softened. They even seemed to be regarding their daughter with a certain amount of sympathy.

"You'd better start cleaning up this mess," Mr. Bailey said quietly, his shoulders sagging as he surveyed the remnants of his dashed hopes.

"Yes, Mr. Bailey," Teddy said with uncharacteristic meekness.

"I'm so sorry," Beatrice said miserably. "Dad—?"

But Mr. Bailey just shook his head and held out a broom. "We'll talk later," he said.

Back at the Witches' Institute, Dr. Aura Featherstone turned off the Magi-monitor. She sat for a long time with her head in her hands.

Unlikely Heroes

"It's probably just as well that I'm magically challenged," Beatrice said fiercely as she swept bits of broken lights into a dustpan. "Otherwise, I'd be *soooo* tempted to turn Amanda Bugg into a hedgehog."

"Yeah," Teddy said, enjoying the image that sprang to mind. "An especially ugly and stupid hedgehog. With no fashion sense whatsoever."

Beatrice sighed. "There's no chance of me turning anybody into anything. I'm a poor excuse of a witch."

"*You* didn't send fifty mortals fleeing for their lives," Teddy pointed out. She sounded depressed. "It's so unfair! The only thing I've ever wanted in my whole life is to be a great witch."

"So you've said," Beatrice replied drily. "A number of times. But we might as well face reality, Teddy. Since our parents are as inept as we are, it must be in the DNA."

Teddy was too preoccupied with her own humiliation to respond. "Is fame and fortune too much to ask for?" she muttered. "Oh, who am I kidding? I'll never be a Classical witch. How can I possibly compete with witches from the

Sphere? They start learning spells in kindergarten at the witch academies."

"And they can practice The Craft openly without hiding their magic from mortals," Beatrice added, "while we have to sneak in a spell when nobody's looking."

"Why did my great-grandparents have to leave the Witches' Sphere and become Reform, anyway?" Teddy continued unhappily. "I need to live among Traditional witches if I ever hope to realize my magical potential."

Beatrice didn't say anything, but she was thinking that maybe she and her friends had already fulfilled whatever potential they had as witches. The prospect was humbling.

"What difference does it make, anyway?" Beatrice demanded suddenly, shoving a charred strand of lights into a trash bag. "I still say—"

"—*that we shouldn't take magic so seriously,*" Teddy finished the sentence for her, mimicking the earnest tone Beatrice used when she tried to convince Teddy that there was nothing wrong with being an Everyday witch.

"You can be *so* annoying," Beatrice said hotly.

"No more than you," Teddy shot back. "The Witches' Executive Committee should have gotten in touch with you by now. But you don't even care that they've forgotten about testing us. In fact," Teddy added, sounding more indignant with every word, "I think you're *glad*. Now you can be an ordinary *Everyday* witch, just like you've always wanted!"

Beatrice's face flooded with color, and Teddy knew instantly that she had said too much.

"Beatrice, I'm sorry," Teddy said quickly. "I didn't mean it. You know me, old Spill-her-guts-first-and-think-about-it-later. I realize I'm selfish, but I promise to do better. Really. From now on—"

"Teddy!" Beatrice gave her a stern look. "Groveling doesn't become you."

Teddy blinked, confused. "Does that mean that you forgive me?" she asked almost timidly.

"It means that I agree that you're hopelessly self-centered," Beatrice said, still irritated enough to enjoy the look of discomfort on her friend's face. "But you probably can't help it. Besides," Beatrice added, a smile tugging at the corners of her mouth despite her best intentions, "if you ever *do* become the greatest witch who ever lived, I want you on my side."

For the first time in days, Teddy laughed.

They had almost finished cleaning when the bell over the front door jingled, and Beatrice looked up in surprise. Was there anyone in town crazy enough to risk bodily injury for a few poinsettias? Then she saw Ollie and Cyrus come through the doorway.

"Should we warn them to steer clear until your parents are feeling better?" Teddy suggested. She glanced warily at the glassed-in office where Mr. and Mrs. Bailey were going over the day's receipts. "Which might not be until next August. They still look pretty upset."

"Teddy, you did run off all their customers," Beatrice reminded her, "who managed to destroy most of the displays on their way out. Then we have those burned spots on the ceiling where the lights exploded. Do you really expect my parents to be *happy* right now?"

The boys had come over to join Beatrice and Teddy, their faces red from the cold and snow glistening in their hair.

"What's all this about lights exploding?" Cyrus wanted to know. He was small and dark, with vivid blue eyes and a good-natured grin.

"Wow. The ceiling doesn't look so good," Ollie said, craning his neck to peer at the peppering of small black craters overhead.

Ollie was nearly as skinny as Beatrice, and several inches taller. He had tousled butter-yellow hair and green eyes that were now resting on Beatrice's face with sympathetic concern.

"What happened?" he asked.

Ollie Tibbs's steady presence always made Beatrice feel better. The fact that he was awfully cute—which she had just started noticing this past year—didn't hurt, either. Beatrice took a deep breath, preparing to tell him and Cyrus about the calamity with the lights, when Teddy took over.

"Haven't you heard?" Teddy demanded. "I thought it would be all over town by now. I cast a spell to hang strands of lights and it blew up in my face."

"Actually," Ollie said thoughtfully, "it looks like they blew up all over the ceiling."

"Were there any mortals here?" Cyrus asked, his eyes unusually bright as he imagined this worst-case scenario.

"Only a couple of hundred," Teddy said sarcastically.

Cyrus's eyes grew brighter and rounder.

"There were no more than thirty," Beatrice said, frowning at Teddy. "Forty tops."

"Ooooh, well then . . ." Cyrus said cheerfully. "Thirty or forty mortal witnesses is nothing to worry about."

Teddy appeared ready to say something scathing in reply, but Ollie spoke first. "This will blow over before you know it," he assured Teddy. "Our problems with mortals always do. And think how disappointed the people in this town would be if they didn't have *some* kind of gossip to spread about us."

While Ollie consoled Teddy, Beatrice noticed that Cyrus was fidgeting more than usual. In fact, he looked like he might explode, himself, if he didn't get to speak up soon.

"Did you guys come to tell us something?" Beatrice guessed.

"I thought you'd never ask!" Cyrus burst out, his grin spreading wider as he began to dig around in his backpack.

"Actually, we came to *show* you something." Ollie spoke calmly, but Beatrice saw an excited sparkle in his eyes.

Cyrus had pulled out a slightly crumpled magazine and was flipping through it to find the right page. "Here it is," he said dramatically, and thrust an article under Beatrice and Teddy's noses.

"*Reform Witches Become Unlikely Heroes,*" Beatrice read the bold headline.

"What is this magazine?" Teddy asked, glancing at the cover. "Oh—*Enchantment News and Witch-world Report,*" she said, and immediately lost interest.

But Beatrice was staring at the color photo beneath the headline. Smiling up at her were Teddy, Ollie, Cyrus, and Beatrice herself, with Cayenne perched on Beatrice's shoulder.

"This is a picture of us," Beatrice said in amazement. "Is that Skull House in the background?"

Now Ollie was grinning. "Yep. It's an article about our trip to the Witches' Sphere and about how we managed to break Dally Rumpe's spell on Winter Wood."

"*What?*" Teddy shrieked. "Let me see that."

"Don't hog it, Teddy," Cyrus protested.

"You're tearing the cover," Ollie said with concern. "My dad hasn't even read it yet."

"I don't remember anyone taking our picture," Beatrice murmured.

They were all grabbing for the magazine and talking at once when Mr. and Mrs. Bailey came out of the office to see what was going on.

"What's so interesting?" Beatrice's father asked them.

"Mr. Bailey, we've made the big time," Cyrus announced. "There's an article about us breaking Dally Rumpe's spell in *Enchantment News*."

Mr. Bailey's face registered astonishment. For once, he appeared speechless. It was Mrs. Bailey who asked sharply, "Where did you get this?"

Hearing the tension in her mother's voice, Beatrice looked up quickly. Nina Bailey's face had turned pale and there was a look of startled wariness in her eyes.

"My parents subscribe," Ollie was saying, smiling. "Comes to the house in a plain brown wrapper and all that."

Mrs. Bailey reached for the magazine. Suddenly everyone stopped talking, watching her. The silence stretched out and became strained. Cyrus shifted uneasily. Teddy and Ollie looked puzzled.

"Mrs. Bailey, are you all right?" Ollie asked quietly.

Nina Bailey was staring at the article and didn't answer. She had that same distant and preoccupied air that Beatrice had noticed at other times over the last few weeks. When Beatrice had mentioned it, Mrs. Bailey had laughed her daughter's concerns aside. But after seeing her mother's reaction to this article, Beatrice could no longer ignore the fact that something was troubling Mrs. Bailey. It had all started, Beatrice realized now, after their trip to the Witches' Sphere.

"Mom, we can read this later," Beatrice said, reaching for the magazine.

"I think," Mrs. Bailey said faintly, "that we should read it now. I don't have my glasses, Hamish. Can you read it to us?"

Beatrice saw uncertainty flash across her father's face, but he recovered quickly. "Of course," Mr. Bailey said. "The headline reads: *Reform Witches Become Unlikely Heroes*."

"*Reform* witches," Teddy muttered. "They *would* have to call attention to that first thing."

"Hush, Teddy," Cyrus chided her. "*Some* people want to hear this."

Teddy looked miffed, but she kept her mouth shut. Mr. Bailey continued to read.

Beatrice Bailiwick, a twelve-year-old Reform witch from the mortal world, has astounded everyone in the Witches' Sphere by reversing the spell cast on Winter Wood, the northern region of what was once the kingdom of Bailiwick. Assisting Ms. Bailiwick in this remarkable magical undertaking were three Reform

friends: Ollie Tibbs, Cyrus Rascallion, and Teddy
Beddy.

"*What!*" Teddy screeched. "Did you read that right? Teddy *Beddy?*" She peered over Mr. Bailey's shoulder to see for herself.

"It's just a typo," Cyrus said impatiently. "Will you please let Mr. Bailey go on?"

"Just a typo?" Teddy stormed. "That's easy for you to say—they spelled *your* name right. No one will even know this is me!"

Mr. Bailey frowned at Teddy, who got the message. He resumed reading.

For all you witches who have forgotten your witch academy history, Bromwich of Bailiwick was a powerful sorcerer who was known for his good works. More than two hundred years ago, the sorcerer Dally Rumpe (who, conversely, is known for his evil deeds) cast a spell to gain control of the kingdom of Bailiwick. Bromwich supporters assert that Dally Rumpe's powers were not strong enough to allow him to take Bailiwick away from Bromwich intact, perhaps explaining why the spell left the kingdom split into five parts. Since that time, Bromwich has been held captive by Dally Rumpe in the central region of Bailiwick. Bromwich's four daughters have been imprisoned in each of the other regions. [For more details on Dally Rumpe's spell, go to our hexsite: Rumpe@enchantmentnews.com]

Beatrice Bailiwick comes from a long line of Bailiwick witches who have attempted to reverse the

*spell and free Bromwich and his daughters. Prior to
Beatrice Bailiwick's success in the northern region,
which resulted in the release of Bromwich's eldest
daughter Rhona, nine witches had attempted to break
the spell and failed.*

*Followers of this fascinating story have not been
able to ascertain how four young Reform witches
could accomplish what older, more experienced
Traditional witches could not. Noted witch scholar,
Most Worthy Piddle, has said of Beatrice Bailiwick,
"I met the witch on her visit to the Sphere, and I
must admit I wasn't overly impressed. She seemed
quite unremarkable and Everyday to me."*

Now it was Beatrice's turn to be steamed. "Well, I
wasn't overly impressed with him," she declared. "He's
so—so—"

"You're spitting, Beatrice," Ollie said, wiping his face
discreetly with the back of his hand.

"So *conceited!*" Beatrice finally blurted out. "The only
person who would ever impress *him* is himself!"

"But he dressed well," Teddy remarked.

Appearing oblivious to the conversation going on
around her, Mrs. Bailey said in a strained voice, "Is there
more, Hamish?"

"Just one paragraph," Mr. Bailey said. Everyone
quieted down, with Beatrice still scowling, while he read.

*Beatrice Bailiwick is the daughter of Hamish
and Nina Bailiwick (née Merriwether), although the
family name was shortened to Bailey when they went*

*Reform. Surprisingly, Ollie Tibbs, who is classified
Everyday, is the great-grandson of illustrious
entrepreneur Sylvestus Tibbs, widely known for
inventing self-spitting toothpaste and invisible
earmuffs. No information is currently available on
Cyrus Rascallion and Teddy Beddy except that they
are Everyday.*

Beatrice looked quickly at Teddy, who was red-faced
but oddly silent.

"Teddy—?" Beatrice began.

"I'm not going to say a thing," Teddy stated haughtily.
"But I promise you this—when I'm rich and famous, I'm
going to buy that rag magazine—and are they ever going
to be sorry!"

"You didn't read the last line, Mr. Bailey," Ollie said.

"Oh?" Mr. Bailey glanced down the page, then his face
went white.

"What is it, Dad?" Beatrice was mildly alarmed.

When Mr. Bailey didn't respond, Beatrice took the
magazine from him. "*Next month's exclusive!*" Beatrice
read. "*Don't miss our in-depth report on Beatrice Bailiwick's
family history and her life among the mortals.*"

"Oh, great," Beatrice muttered. "Witch reporters
snooping around aren't going to call attention to me or
anything, are they?"

Then Beatrice's eyes fell on her mother's face. Mrs.
Bailey's paleness had turned to a grayish pallor. "Mom—?"

"Why don't you go home?" Nina Bailey said. The
words came out sounding harsh. "You—*you all*—deserve to
have some fun on your vacation," she added more gently.

Then Mrs. Bailey turned abruptly, and with purposeful intent, walked to the office and closed the door behind her.

Beatrice started after her mother, but Mr. Bailey caught his daughter's arm. "I'll see about her," he said softly. "Go have a good time with your friends."

After Mr. Bailey had left, there was a brief uncomfortable silence. Mrs. Bailey was the one adult Beatrice's friends could usually count on to be upbeat and fun, and her reaction to the article had perplexed them all.

Suddenly Teddy burst out, "It's all my fault! Beatrice, I didn't realize how much I upset your mother with that stupid light spell. How can I make it up to her?"

Brows furrowed in thought, Beatrice blew her bangs out of her eyes. "It wasn't the spell that made her—act like that." Then Beatrice stopped. Because she had no other explanation for her mother's odd behavior. Something about the Witches' Sphere—and apparently, the promised exposé on Beatrice's family—had upset her.

"I'm sure she was worried about you while we were in the Sphere," Ollie said to Beatrice, "and now she's afraid we'll be going back."

"Fat chance," Teddy said flatly. "Has anyone seen a certain witch committee lurking around lately?"

"Do you want to talk to your mom before we leave?" Ollie asked Beatrice.

She thought about it, then shook her head. "No. I'll see her at home later."

Beatrice and Teddy were putting on their coats when the first shopper arrived, soon followed by another, and then another. Before long, the nursery was crowded with people, all appearing strangely cheerful and excited.

Beatrice gawked at them. "What in the *world?*" she muttered.

Mr. Bailey looked equally puzzled when he came out of his office and saw the aisles once again teeming with customers.

"May I help you?" he asked when a man approached him.

"I'd like some of those lights you demonstrated earlier," the customer replied. "You know, the ones that shoot off like fireworks."

"I came for those, too," said the woman behind him. "They must be the newest thing."

Then all the shoppers were pressing in on Mr. Bailey, requesting those incredibly unique and amusing skyrocket lights.

Mr. Bailey just stared at them with his mouth open as they grew more animated and more insistent in their demands. Watching all this in amazement, Beatrice began to laugh.

"Teddy, I guess you're off the hook," Beatrice said with a grin. "But you're going to be kept pretty busy filling all these orders."

"Don't even joke about it," Teddy groaned.

Then they heard Mr. Bailey shouting over the roar of voices. "We're sold out! Do you hear me? *No*, we don't have any more! Try us again next year."

What strange people mortals are, Beatrice thought, as she pulled Cayenne's woolly sweater over the cat's head. *I'll never understand them if I live to be five hundred.*

Cayenne leaped to Beatrice's shoulder and they followed the others outside into the cold twilight. A blast of wind and snow hit Beatrice in the face as she sank knee-deep into a drift outside the door.

"You forgot to turn it off," Teddy said.

Beatrice quickly mumbled a spell. The snow stopped falling, but two feet of the stuff was already on the ground. It was going to be a long walk home.

"Ollie," Cyrus said as they trudged down the street, "can you help us out with your boiling water spell?"

"Sure," Ollie replied, and began to chant:

> *Heat of flame, heat of fire,*
> *Give to me my one desire.*
> *Melt the snow that we now see,*
> *As my will, so mote it be!*

Boiling water began to bubble alongside the curbs, melting the snow and then swirling down the sewer drains.

In the paper the following morning, the headline read: *Blizzard Catches Downtown Unprepared.* Beatrice scanned the article over breakfast.

> *Twenty-one inches of snow covered a two-block area*
> *from Main Avenue to Second Street. Meteorologist*
> *Scott Badcall terms it a freak event, which could*
> *have been caused by any number of meteorological*
> *conditions. Badcall declined to elaborate.*

3

A Circle of Witches

Beatrice woke up suddenly. She had been dreaming about her mother—and another woman that she seemed to know but couldn't identify—so when she heard the murmur of women's voices, Beatrice thought at first that she was still dreaming.

Then the clock in the downstairs hall struck twenty-three, startling Beatrice out of her drowsy half sleep. That's when she knew that the voices were real. They seemed to be coming through the heat vent from the living room.

Beatrice slipped out of her warm bed and shivered when her feet touched the icy hardwood floor. As usual, the furnace in the old house was rumbling and groaning in an effort to do its work, but without much success. Beatrice shoved her feet into fuzzy green dragon slippers and snatched up her robe as she groped her way through the darkness to the hallway.

Light from the moon poured through the window on the landing, illuminating the stairwell. Beatrice started down the stairs, intent on finding out who was meeting in her living room so late at night. And in the dark, at that. Since, in her opinion, the situation was odd enough to warrant surreptitious investigation, Beatrice tried not to make any noise. But halfway down, a board squeaked under her foot. Beatrice froze. She listened for a full minute as the muffled conversation continued on without interruption, and then resumed her stealthy descent to the downstairs hall.

As she approached the doorway to the living room, Beatrice recognized her mother's voice. Beatrice couldn't quite hear what Nina Bailey was saying, but there was an urgency in her tone that made Beatrice uneasy. Then another woman was speaking. The voice sounded vaguely familiar.

Beatrice edged closer to the door and peered into the dark room. Her mother paced back and forth in front of a moon-bright window. The other woman stood nearby, her face averted and hidden in shadow. But cold silver light fell across the woman's shoulder, revealing red tones in the dark hair and casting a frosty sheen on the green silk robes. In a shocked instant, Beatrice knew who was there talking to her mother. It was Aura Featherstone!

Beatrice ducked back from the doorway, her heart pounding against her ribs. Questions swirled inside her head until she felt light-headed. What was Dr Featherstone doing here so late at night? Why was she talking to Beatrice's mother? And why were they being so secretive, meeting in the dark and practically whispering? Except that now her mother's voice was becoming louder and more agitated.

Beatrice lowered herself to the floor and tried to make her rapid breathing return to normal. She had seen Dr. Featherstone only twice in her life. The first time was at her twelfth birthday party, when all thirteen members of the Witches' Executive Committee had shown up—not to give Beatrice the Everyday classification she had expected, but to tell her that she wouldn't be classified at all until she was tested. The second time was in the Witches' Sphere, after Beatrice and her friends had returned from Winter Wood and were being honored for breaking Dally Rumpe's spell. Both times, Beatrice had had the feeling that Aura Featherstone was cheering for her, that she really *wanted* Beatrice to succeed.

Dr. Featherstone had told Beatrice that the committee would let her know when it was time for the second part of the test. But that had been nearly two months ago, and Beatrice had begun to think that she had seen the last of the witch committee. In all honesty, she had secretly *hoped* this was the case—because she had mixed feelings about the whole Everyday–Classical witch thing. She wouldn't mind being a more capable witch, but unlike Teddy, Beatrice had never even considered the possibility of being classified Classical. She knew that her magical powers were limited—which only made their success in Winter Wood all the more astonishing. Beatrice still didn't know how they had managed to win out over a powerful sorcerer like Dally Rumpe. But they had, and now everyone would assume that they could do it again. The pressure of trying to live up to such high expectations frightened Beatrice more than the prospect of facing Dally Rumpe again.

Beatrice's heart had slowed down and was no longer thumping in her ears. She pressed her face against the wall and listened.

"—and she has a happy life," Beatrice's mother was saying emphatically, perhaps with a hint of desperation in her voice.

"I'm sure she has," Aura Featherstone answered calmly. "But, Nina, what right do you have to deny Beatrice her destiny?"

Nina? Beatrice sat back, feeling more confused than ever. Did her mother and Dr. Featherstone know each other?

"I have *every* right to protect my daughter," Mrs. Bailey snapped. "And I, of all people, know how easy it is to become enchanted by the Witches' Sphere and lose all perspective."

"But you were given the chance to make your own decision," Aura Featherstone responded mildly. "Doesn't Beatrice deserve the same opportunity?"

"You don't know how hard it was while she was there," Mrs. Bailey burst out. "I was terrified the whole time. A girl her age up against that kind of evil! And when she came home safely, I told myself that I would never agree to let her go again. Especially . . ."

"Especially to the southern part of the Sphere," Dr. Featherstone finished quietly.

"That's right. I won't have Beatrice going anywhere near Friar's Lantern."

"Nina, you're letting your own history and personal feelings get in the way. Shouldn't Beatrice be allowed to meet her family?"

"*No!*" Mrs. Bailey cried out. "They'll try to convince her to stay, just as they did with me."

"But you left."

"*I ran away!*"

There was anguish in Nina Bailey's voice, and Beatrice felt the impulse to go to her. But then Beatrice remembered that she wasn't even supposed to be hearing this conversation and stayed where she was.

"I ran," Mrs. Bailey repeated dully, "but Beatrice might decide differently. You know I can never return to the Sphere, even to visit her. I can't lose my daughter!"

Beatrice heard weeping. When she looked into the room again, she saw Dr. Featherstone holding her mother while Nina Bailey cried. *You'll never lose me*, Beatrice vowed silently. There was only one reason why she felt compelled to go back to the Witches' Sphere, and that was to help Bromwich and his daughters. They were family, and they were counting on her. Beatrice had thought her mother understood that.

Beatrice leaned back limply against the wall. None of this made any sense. Her mother had been to the Witches' Sphere? Then why had she never mentioned it? And why had she run away? It came as a profound shock to Beatrice to realize that her mother had a past that she, Beatrice, knew nothing about.

The weeping stopped, and then Aura Featherstone said firmly, but not without sympathy, "The Witches' Executive Committee has made its decision. Beatrice and her friends will return to the Witches' Sphere in two days' time. The committee will be here at the stroke of midnight

33

to give Beatrice her instructions. But I wanted to tell you first, so it wouldn't come as such a shock."

"How considerate," Mrs. Bailey said sarcastically.

"Blesséd be!" Aura Featherstone's words came out as a small explosion. "You were the most headstrong young witch I ever knew, Nina Merriwether! No one could tell you anything. I tried to make you think about the possible consequences before you left the Sphere, but you wouldn't listen."

"I've had a good life here," Mrs. Bailey said defensively. "If I hadn't come back, I wouldn't have Hamish or Beatrice. I'd never give them up! Not for all the power in the Witches' Sphere."

"But *you* made that decision. Isn't Beatrice entitled to do the same?"

Beatrice heard a deep sigh, followed by a lengthy silence. Finally, Nina Bailey asked hoarsely, "When will the committee be arriving?"

"Soon," Aura Featherstone answered. "Why don't you wake Beatrice and bring her down?"

That was Beatrice's cue to scramble to her feet and run back upstairs. She kicked off her slippers and hopped into bed, prepared to feign sleep when her mother came in.

But Mrs. Bailey went first to wake her husband. Beatrice heard them whispering, then the creaking of the floor as the two of them entered her room.

Mr. Bailey turned on the lamp beside the bed.

Mrs. Bailey shook her daughter gently. "Beatrice, the Witches' Executive Committee is waiting for you downstairs."

Beatrice made a show of being sleepy and confused as she got out of bed and searched for her slippers. She longed to tell her mother that she would never leave her life here, no matter what. But Mrs. Bailey was already out the door.

Cayenne leaped from the bed to Beatrice's shoulder. The two of them followed Beatrice's parents down the stairs and into the living room—where a circle of thirteen witches waited.

Each of the witches held a lit candle. The rich colors of their jewel-tone robes and pointed hats shimmered in the flickering light. There was Dr. Featherstone in jade green and Dr. Meadowmouse in royal purple. Both were smiling at Beatrice. The other witches' expressions suggested extreme boredom.

The only witch dressed in black came forward to stand in front of Beatrice. He had once been tall, but was now stooped with age. Beatrice looked into the pale blue eyes of Thaddeus Thigpin, Director of the Witches' Institute, and knew that his attitude toward her hadn't changed a bit. He was just as convinced as he had been two months ago that he and the other members of the committee were wasting their time with Beatrice, a lowly Reform witch with little talent for magic.

Dr. Thigpin stared hard at Beatrice, his eyes no more than icy slits beneath a ridge of shaggy white brows. Then he said in the deep powerful voice that Beatrice remembered, "The time has come for the second part of your test."

Beatrice nodded, determined not to lose her composure under his cold scrutiny.

Then Dr. Thigpin made a noise deep in his throat, a growl of impatience, perhaps, and added, "We've been through this before, so you know the drill." He glanced behind him, where Drs. Featherstone and Meadowmouse stood together. "I assume the two of you can carry on without any assistance from me."

"Of course, Thaddeus," Dr. Featherstone murmured.

"Then the rest of us shall return to the institute and leave Ms.—er—*Bailiwick*—in your very capable hands," Dr. Thigpin said stiffly. And just like that, eleven of the thirteen committee witches were gone.

Now Beatrice could see Peregrine, her witch adviser, standing behind a potted fern. She smiled at him and he ducked his head, the corners of his small mouth lifting slightly.

He was dressed in the mole brown robes that he always wore. No more than four feet tall, with very large ears that stuck out like bat wings from his toast-colored hair, Peregrine did little to instill confidence in a young witch in need of guidance. But on their trip to the Witches' Sphere, Beatrice had become fond of her timid witch adviser.

Dr. Featherstone came to stand with Beatrice, followed by Dr. Meadowmouse, who had taken hold of Peregrine's sleeve and was dragging the reluctant witch adviser from his hiding place.

"It's good to see you again, Beatrice," Aura Featherstone said warmly.

"As Dr. Thigpin phrased it, you know the drill," Dr. Meadowmouse said to Beatrice with a humorous twist of his mouth. "However, we are required to explain the entire test to you again before you embark on the second part." Seeing Beatrice's look of dismay, he added quickly, "At least the high points. All right, shall we begin?"

Dr. Meadowmouse looked over at a thick black book that lay closed on the desk. Its binding was cracked and faded with age. Suddenly the book sailed across the room into Dr. Meadowmouse's hands. As it fell open, several large black beetles crawled out and dropped to the floor.

"Beatrice, as you know," Dr. Meadowmouse said, "we have here *The Bailiwick Family History*. As you also know, you are related to a very wise and powerful sorcerer named Bromwich of Bailiwick who has been held captive for two hundred years by the evil sorcerer Dally Rumpe."

"Yes," Beatrice said, "I know that."

"And we talked before about how Dally Rumpe's spell caused the kingdom of Bailiwick to split into five parts," Dr. Meadowmouse went on. "He somehow managed to upset the delicate balance of the four basic elements needed to sustain life. Do you remember what those elements are?" he asked, seeming for the moment like a kindly witch tutor, hoping that his favorite student would be a star.

"Earth," Beatrice said, to the expectant nods of Drs. Meadowmouse and Featherstone, "air, water, and—" She didn't think she knew the fourth one and felt a moment of panic. Then it came to her. "Fire," Beatrice finished triumphantly, and the two witches' eyes sparkled with delight.

"That's correct!" Dr. Meadowmouse said. "The central region of Bailiwick, where Bromwich is imprisoned in his own castle, has remained essentially unchanged. But in each of the other regions, Dally Rumpe's spell caused one of the four basic elements to become dominant, resulting in a land of extremes."

At this point, Dr. Featherstone couldn't resist putting her two cents in. "Beatrice, I'm sure you recall that air was the dominant element in Winter Wood. That's why the region was buried in ice and snow year-round and the people were living on the edge of starvation. That is," she added, with a sudden radiant smile, "until you and your friends broke the spell on Winter Wood and freed Bromwich's daughter Rhona."

"Who is quite happy now," Dr. Meadowmouse broke in, obviously annoyed that his colleague had tried to upstage him. "Except, of course, for being concerned about her father and sisters. When you reversed the spell, the snow melted away and Dally Rumpe melted with it. He can never set foot in that part of Bailiwick again. But he still has control of the other four regions."

"Which is why we're here," Aura Featherstone said. "It's time for you to go to the southern part of Bailiwick. To Werewolf Close."

Dr. Meadowmouse frowned at Dr. Featherstone. "I wanted to say that part, Aura."

"Sorry," Dr. Featherstone murmured, but she didn't appear to be sorry at all. Beatrice thought she looked excited, like she couldn't wait to name all the perils that Beatrice would face in this werewolf place. And wasn't that a pleasant name? *Werewolf Close.* Beatrice resisted a shudder.

"The dominant element in the south is earth," Dr. Meadowmouse told Beatrice. "Werewolf Close is always extremely hot. The sun never sets and it hardly ever rains, so crops die and the people suffer terribly."

"And let me guess," Beatrice said. "It's guarded by werewolves."

"That's correct," Dr. Meadowmouse answered, frowning as he studied a passage in the book. "Enchanted fog encircles the region. The fog is three miles wide and no one can enter it without becoming disoriented and losing all sense of direction. Except for the werewolves," he added, glancing at Beatrice, then looking down at the book again. "They wait to attack anyone who tries to come through the fog."

Great, Beatrice thought. This place was sounding like so much fun already.

"Bromwich's second daughter, Innes, is held captive by Dally Rumpe inside Werewolf Close," Dr. Meadowmouse went on. "She's guarded by a vicious manticore."

"Oh," Beatrice said. Then, "What is—?"

"A manticore," Dr. Featherstone finished, as if she had been waiting for that question. "It's a very fierce creature about the size of—" she appeared to be searching for a comparison that would mean something to Beatrice "—a large horse, although its body, tail, and claws are more like a lion. It has a man's head, very long fangs, a flowing lion's mane, and two sharp horns above its ears."

"And don't forget the dragon's wings," Dr. Meadowmouse reminded her. "Oh, yes, and it speaks as we do—has perfect diction, in fact—but its voice sounds like the tones of a flute and a trumpet playing at once."

Beatrice couldn't even imagine this creature, but it sounded perfectly horrible. She glanced at her mother to see how she was taking it all so far. Mrs. Bailey's mouth was set in a thin line and she was squinting as if she had a headache. Beatrice's father looked tired and worried.

"Your purpose in Werewolf Close will be the same as before," Dr. Meadowmouse said. "After you've found Innes, you must repeat the spell written here—" he thumped the book with his knuckle "—in her presence. Once you've done that, the extreme heat will go away, crops will grow, Innes will be free, and Dally Rumpe will be banished from the region forever."

"You're to leave day after tomorrow," Dr. Featherstone told Beatrice. "And Peregrine will accompany you."

"Where will they stay?"

Beatrice was startled to hear her mother speak and spun around to look at her.

"That's being—arranged," Dr. Featherstone replied.

"I'll bet it is," Mrs. Bailey said under her breath, but Beatrice heard her.

Dr. Featherstone's chin rose a fraction and she stared at Beatrice's mother. "What was that you said, Mrs. Bailey?" she asked with cool courtesy.

Nina Bailey just shook her head and stared at the floor. Meanwhile, Dr. Meadowmouse had turned to Peregrine. "Will you show Beatrice the map please?" he asked the witch adviser.

Peregrine pulled a sheet of rolled-up parchment from inside his robes, which he then spread out across the top of the desk.

Beatrice went over and studied the map. It looked just like the one Peregrine had shown them before the trip to Winter Wood. *Except . . .* Beatrice picked up the map to examine the lower right-hand corner more closely. Yes, something had been added. Southeast of Werewolf Close was a cluster of buildings that hadn't been there before. And beneath the buildings was printed *Friar's Lantern*.

The words leaped out at Beatrice, and her heart began to beat very fast. *I won't have Beatrice going anywhere near Friar's Lantern*, her mother had said. But here it was on the map, so Beatrice assumed that the Executive Committee meant for them to go there.

Beatrice placed the map back on the desk and looked up to find Dr. Featherstone watching her expectantly. *She's waiting for me to ask about Friar's Lantern*, Beatrice thought. And Beatrice wanted to—her curiosity about the place was enormous—but she knew this would only upset her mother more. Beatrice decided that her questions could wait.

"Here is Werewolf Close," Dr. Meadowmouse said, pointing at the map.

"Yes, I see," was all Beatrice said. And then turning to Peregrine, she added, "You know, I've looked under the blackberry bushes out back for the tunnel we took to the Witches' Sphere. But it isn't there anymore."

"Of course not." Peregrine seemed surprised that she would have expected it to be. "We change routes to the Sphere all the time. Can't have just any Tom, Dick, or hobgoblin wandering in whenever they please."

Dr. Meadowmouse nodded his solemn agreement.

"Travel light," Peregrine said to Beatrice. "Take summer clothing and good walking shoes."

"One more thing, Beatrice," Dr. Featherstone said. "Have you read *The Bailiwick Family History* recently?"

"Not since I had to memorize the counterspell for our trip," Beatrice admitted.

"You might want to," Aura Featherstone said casually, "since you're mentioned in it."

That got Beatrice's attention. "I am?"

Dr. Featherstone smiled. "Oh, yes. It talks about the spell being broken on Winter Wood by Beatrice, Witch of Bailiwick. You're part of your official family history now."

All Beatrice could think was, *Wow*.

"Your three friends will be going with you, I suppose," Dr. Meadowmouse said.

"Yes, of course," Beatrice replied.

Dr. Meadowmouse seemed to be writing that down in a tiny book he had produced from a pocket inside his robes. "And your cat-familiar," he murmured.

Then he glanced at the plump owl-eyed cat on Beatrice's shoulder—who at the moment was simply staring blankly into space—and looked doubtful.

"Well . . ." Dr. Meadowmouse said, and went back to his writing.

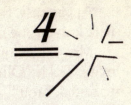

4

The Merriwethers

Beatrice slept late the next morning and was still in her nightgown and robe when she came down for breakfast. Her parents were sitting at the kitchen table drinking coffee.

"Oh, good, you're up," Mrs. Bailey said when she saw Beatrice. "I thought I'd make waffles. Would you like that?"

Beatrice was surprised by her mother's apparent cheerfulness. In fact, Mrs. Bailey seemed almost like her old self—except for the purple smudges under her eyes that suggested she hadn't slept much the night before.

"Waffles sound great," Beatrice said, sitting down across from her father.

Actually, Mrs. Bailey's idea of making waffles was taking a box out of the freezer and zapping its contents in the microwave. Even so, what she typically served up had the consistency of a doormat. Mrs. Bailey wasn't much of a cook. But Beatrice was so relieved to see her mother behaving normally, she would happily choke down whatever Nina Bailey set in front of her.

Apparently, Beatrice's father felt the same. "I'll get the steak knives," he murmured.

Mrs. Bailey opened the freezer door. "Why don't you invite Teddy, Ollie, and Cyrus over for breakfast?" she suggested. "You'll want to tell them about your trip to the Witches' Sphere."

Beatrice and Mr. Bailey exchanged a look. He gave her a discreet nod.

"Okay," Beatrice said, getting up from the table. "I'll go call them."

Her friends were so excited by the news that they were even willing to endure Mrs. Bailey's cooking. They said they'd be right over.

Beatrice ran upstairs and changed into jeans and a sweater. When she came back to the kitchen, she saw that her mother had been hard at work. There were stacks of waffles lined up on every counter. Cayenne was wrestling with one under the table, pressing it to the floor with her front paws while she tried without much success to gnaw off a corner. The cat looked like she was about to break out into a sweat.

Beatrice's mother seemed unaware that she had fixed enough waffles to feed half the town and was shoving more into the microwave. Beatrice gave her father a worried look. Mr. Bailey shrugged and then sighed.

"Cyrus always has a healthy appetite," he remarked.

Beatrice heard footsteps and voices on the front porch. "They're here," she said, and went to let them in.

When Beatrice opened the front door, she was greeted by the flushed faces of her three friends.

"It's about time the committee came through!" Teddy exclaimed.

"Yeah," Cyrus agreed, "we need an adventure. It was getting pretty boring around here."

Ever practical, Ollie said thoughtfully, "It's convenient that the trip coincides with Winter Break." But Beatrice detected a gleam of anticipation in his eyes.

"Come on in," Beatrice said. "I hope you haven't eaten in a couple of days."

As Teddy, Ollie, and Cyrus trooped into the front hall, Beatrice saw the mail carrier coming up the walk. She went outside to meet him.

"Good morning, Beatrice," he said, handing her a thick bundle of mail. His eyes glittered as he added, "I heard you had quite a show over at the nursery the other day—lights shooting off like rockets."

"It was my dad's idea," Beatrice said hastily, and grabbed the mail from him. "Thanks, Mr. Winkum. Have a good day."

Leaving a disappointed mailman to stare after her, Beatrice hurried up the steps, pretending to be absorbed in the ton of catalogs and credit-card offers he had delivered. She was about to go inside when something caught her eye. An envelope was sticking out of the mailbox beside the door.

That's odd, Beatrice thought. She had met Mr. Winkum before he had time to reach the mailbox, and she clearly remembered bringing in yesterday's mail.

Beatrice lifted the mailbox lid and withdrew a lavender envelope that resembled a greeting card. Her heart began to thump as she stared down at the purple handwriting on the front of the envelope. It was addressed to Ms. *Beatrice Bailiwick* and was postmarked from the Witches' Sphere.

Beatrice joined the others in the kitchen. Her friends and Mr. Bailey were sitting around the table while Mrs. Bailey poured syrup over Teddy's waffles. Cayenne was lying on the floor, apparently exhausted, using her waffle as a pillow.

"Oh, the mail came," Mr. Bailey said, and Beatrice handed him everything except the letter addressed to her.

"What's that?" Mrs. Bailey had stopped pouring and was staring at the lavender envelope in Beatrice's hand.

Beatrice steeled herself for her mother's reaction. "It's for me, from the Witches' Sphere." She peered down at the return address, which was rather scrawled and hard to read. "It's from—I think it's *Primrose and* . . . something . . . *Merriwether*."

"Primrose and Laurel Merriwether," Mrs. Bailey said. She spoke calmly, her face expressionless, and Beatrice knew that her mother had been expecting this.

Beatrice looked back at the envelope. "*Primrose and Laurel Merriwether*," she read aloud, "*7 Muttering Lane*—" And then she stopped, glancing at her mother again.

"*Friar's Lantern*," Mrs. Bailey finished softly.

Mr. Bailey was also looking at his wife. "Your aunts," he said, his voice strangely flat.

Beatrice turned her attention to him. So he had known that Nina Bailey had family in the Sphere, which was more than Beatrice could say. She felt a twinge of annoyance. What was the big secret, anyway?

"I thought—uh—" Mr. Bailey fumbled for the right words. "Are they allowed to write to you?" he asked his wife.

"They didn't," Mrs. Bailey answered. She gave her daughter a small strained smile. "They wrote to Beatrice. That *is* allowed."

Beatrice's friends sat motionless, their expressions a mixture of eagerness and confusion as they looked from Beatrice to Mrs. Bailey.

"Open your letter," Mrs. Bailey said to Beatrice. "Don't you want to know what your great-aunts have to say?"

Beatrice hesitated, then nodded. The others watched in silence as she tore open the envelope and pulled out folded lavender stationary.

"Read it aloud," Teddy said, then caught herself. "I mean—if you don't mind us hearing it."

Feeling stunned by everything that had happened since she had discovered Aura Featherstone in her living room, Beatrice said, "I don't mind," and began to read.

Dearest Beatrice,

No doubt this letter will come as a surprise, but we feel that it's long past time to introduce ourselves. I am your Great-aunt Primrose, and your Great-aunt Laurel is helping me compose this letter. We live in a little village in the Witches' Sphere called Friar's Lantern.

You may think this is a strange name for a village, but it is really quite logical and descriptive. We live in the low country, and on clear nights we

*often see faint lights moving across the bogs and
marshes. Some say the lights are lanterns carried by
evildoers as they lead their victims into the dangerous
swamps. In any case, the lights have been here as
long as anyone can remember, and they are called by
any number of different names, most often, fox fire,
fools fire, will-o'-the-wisp, and the friar's lantern.*

Beatrice looked up at her mother. Mrs. Bailey still
appeared calm, almost stoic. "Go on," she said.

*You cannot imagine, dear Beatrice, how
proud of you your Aunt Laurel and I are. The
entire Witches' Sphere has been all atwitter since
Halloween, when a young Reform witch named
Beatrice Bailiwick marched herself in here and did
what no one else has been able to do. Everyone in
the Sphere is talking about how you and your three
brave friends have created such amazing magic.*

Now Beatrice looked to see how Teddy, Ollie, and
Cyrus were responding to the praise. As she might have
expected, they all had silly grins on their faces.

*We have heard through the witches' grapevine
that you four will be coming to this part of the Sphere
very soon. You must stay with us, Beatrice. We are
so anxious to get to know you, and we want you to
learn about the Merriwethers. Also, there is good
magic in Friar's Lantern that will keep you safe.
Perhaps your mother has spoken to you about us,*

48

*and about why we haven't been able to be a part of
your life. But either way, please tell her that we love
her, and that we will do everything in our power to
take good care of her daughter.*

*Do say that you will come to Friar's Lantern,
and tell your friends that they will be most welcome,
as well.*

Blesséd be.

Your loving aunts,

Primrose & Laurel Merriwether

No one spoke for a moment. Then Teddy blurted out,
"I want to stay with them, Beatrice! Just think, we'd be
living with Traditional witches in a Traditional witch village. We *have* to go to Friar's Lantern!"

Mrs. Bailey's eyes clouded slightly. Then a look of
resolve settled over her face, and she said, "You should
accept the aunts' invitation, Beatrice. It's true what they
say—they would slay a dragon, if need be, to keep you from
harm."

"What about a werewolf?" Cyrus piped up, grinning. When no one laughed, he blushed and lowered
his eyes to the stack of waffles that sat untouched in front
of him.

Beatrice felt torn and confused. "Why didn't you ever
tell me that you'd lived in the Witches' Sphere?" she
demanded.

"Because that would have meant telling you other
things," Mrs. Bailey said vaguely, "things I wasn't prepared
to share with you."

"But surely now—" Beatrice began.

"No." Mrs. Bailey shook her head as if to clear it of burdensome thoughts. "It doesn't matter, Beatrice. None of it has anything to do with you."

Before Beatrice could respond, Mrs. Bailey stood up and headed for the microwave. "More waffles anyone?" she asked brightly.

5

Return to the Witches' Sphere

The morning they were to leave for the Witches' Sphere was cold and damp. When Beatrice and her friends walked out to the porch, bundled up in thick jackets and their warmest hats and gloves, Ollie sniffed the air and said, "I think it's going to snow."

"There won't be any snow where we're going," Cyrus declared.

Mr. Bailey came out carrying Beatrice's backpack, followed by Mrs. Bailey who had bag lunches for everyone. For the past two days, Beatrice's mother had been almost painfully cheerful as she helped her daughter pack, always carefully avoiding any discussion of her life in the Witches' Sphere. Beatrice had finally stopped asking about it. But if she accomplished nothing else on this trip, Beatrice was determined to find out why Nina Bailey had left the Sphere, and why she could never go back.

A pale ribbon of light was just beginning to show above the horizon when Peregrine suddenly appeared on the front steps. Beatrice blinked. She still hadn't gotten used to these witches from the Sphere just popping up out of nowhere.

Peregrine was wearing the same dull brown robes, but he had added winter accessories: a red-and-gold striped stocking cap that pressed his hair flat and made his ears appear enormous, and a pair of bright orange mittens.

Good-byes were short. Mrs. Bailey seemed to have planned it that way. She handed out lunches, gave Beatrice a massive hug, cautioned them to be careful, and went back into the house. Mr. Bailey kissed Beatrice on the cheek and murmured, "We'll see you soon, sweetheart. Don't take any unnecessary risks!" before following his wife inside.

Beatrice stowed Cayenne in the pocket of her backpack, so that only the cat's head was visible, and they were off. Peregrine led the way around the house, as he had before. Only this time they went past the blackberry bushes and straight into Mrs. Duvall's backyard.

This was a woman who didn't like people tromping on her grass, especially Beatrice—because, as she had told anyone who would listen, "The Baileys are just plain weird." Cutting across Mrs. Duvall's property made Beatrice uncomfortable. In fact, she couldn't shake the feeling that someone's eyes were following them every step of the way.

Beatrice turned around to Teddy, who was just behind her. "I'm probably being paranoid, but I think we're being watched."

"I'll do my spell and find out," Teddy said. Then she began to chant:

Candle, bell, and willow tree,
Who does snoop and spy on me?
Use your magic for our side,
Show us who would wish to hide.

Suddenly, the curtains at Mrs. Duvall's kitchen window flew open, revealing a woman whose startled expression was framed by bright pink hair curlers. From the way she was bent over with her nose pressed against the glass, Beatrice knew that Mrs. Duvall had been peering at them through a slit in the curtains. *More neighborhood gossip about the Baileys*, Beatrice thought with a sigh. Mrs. Duvall would be telling everyone how she had seen Beatrice and her friends being led away by a little man in a brown bathrobe and orange mittens.

They followed Peregrine across the street and into the woods. Soon Beatrice could see the sparkle of early morning sunlight on water, and she knew they were headed for the river.

Peregrine led them through the trees and undergrowth to a narrow beach that ran alongside the water. They trudged through the sand until they came to an old pier that looked as if it had been abandoned. A boat was docked there. As they started down the pier, Beatrice could see two men sitting in the back of the boat, their hands resting loosely on the oars.

"That's ours," Peregrine said, pointing to the boat.

Beatrice noted how small it was. She didn't think they would all fit. And it was so old and rickety, she wondered if it would actually float. And those men! Scowls appeared to be permanently etched on their weathered faces, and they looked older than the boat. Beatrice wasn't at all sure this was going to work out.

No one spoke as they followed Peregrine to the end of the pier.

"Well, here we are," the witch adviser announced.

"This boat looks like it went down with the *Titanic*," Ollie said bluntly.

"But it's probably a magic boat," Teddy said quickly, so determined to get to the Witches' Sphere, she was prepared to swim if she had to. "And magic boats won't sink. It's magic, right, Peregrine?"

"Well—no," Peregrine said. "Actually, I bought it at the flea market."

Beatrice grinned. "And I bet you got these guys at a two-for-one sale," she said.

But Peregrine didn't see the humor in her remark. The tips of his ears turned pink and one of his eyes began to twitch. "You may not realize this," he said, his bottom lip quivering slightly, "but they don't give me much of a budget. I don't even have an expense account."

Beatrice hadn't meant to hurt Peregrine's feelings. She looked at her witch adviser's wounded expression, and said, "Just kidding." But as she stepped into the boat, Beatrice fully expected it to sink like a bag of sand.

It didn't. Pleasantly surprised, Beatrice smiled politely at the grimacing men with the oars. They ignored her.

Teddy came next and sat down on the middle seat plank beside Beatrice. Ollie and Cyrus took the plank in front. Cayenne could perch on Beatrice's backpack in the floor of the boat, but there was no place for Peregrine to sit.

"I can fix this," Cyrus said. He started to chant:

> *By the mysteries, one and all,*
> *Make me shrink from tall to small.*
> *Cut me down to inches three,*
> *As my will, so mote it be.*

Instantly, Cyrus began to shrink smaller and smaller, until he was only three inches tall. He hopped up on Beatrice's backpack beside Cayenne and offered Peregrine the seat beside Ollie.

Cayenne stared down at Cyrus with her round green-gold eyes and promptly began to lick his head. After a few swipes from her grainy tongue, Cyrus's face looked raw and his hair was dripping wet.

"*Puh-lease!*" Cyrus protested.

The men lowered their oars into the water and the boat began to move. As they made their way down the river, Beatrice noticed the sky becoming darker. Soon the faces of her companions began to blur and then fade into their gray surroundings.

Teddy said loudly over her shoulder, "Hey, you guys in the back! Can you see how to steer this thing?"

"What's happened to the sun?" Beatrice asked Peregrine.

"We've entered The Borderlands," Peregrine replied, "the region between the mortal world and the Witches' Sphere. When we get closer to the Sphere, things will brighten up."

Floating through the darkness with no idea where they were going made Beatrice jittery. She felt around

with her foot to see if water was leaking into the boat, an
struck something solid.

"*Watch it!*" Cyrus yelled out.

"Sorry," Beatrice mumbled.

The air around them was growing warmer. Beatric
took off her gloves, then her heavy jacket. She coul
hear movement around her that suggested the others wer
doing the same.

The farther they traveled downriver, the warmer an
heavier the air became. Before long, Beatrice was pullin
off her hat and using it to wipe perspiration from her fac

"It's so muggy," Teddy complained. "I can't stan
sweating."

"Something tells me we'd better get used to it," Olli
said. "Why don't we have lunch to pass the time?"

They opened the bags Mrs. Bailey had given them an
ate in silence. Beatrice broke off bits of her tuna sandwic
for Cayenne and Cyrus.

"I feel like somebody's pet," Cyrus grumbled. He too
another bite of tuna from Beatrice, and added, "Actuall
it's not so bad."

After everyone had finished eating, Beatrice collecte
the trash and shoved it into her backpack. When sh
looked up again, she realized that she could make ou
the shapes of trees and bushes along the riverbank. "It
becoming lighter," she said.

"We're getting close to the Witches' Sphere,
Peregrine replied.

Before long, the sun eased above the trees, its re
flected glare off the water nearly blinding them. Beatric
mopped at her face with her jacket and put her hat bac

to shade her eyes. She dangled her fingers into the
water and discovered that it was refreshingly cool.

"Don't do that!" Peregrine said sharply.

Beatrice jerked her hand back. "Why not?"

"We're approaching the swamps," Peregrine said, more
gently. "You never know what might be lurking down
here."

Beatrice glanced anxiously over the side of the boat,
seeing nothing but smooth green water. Trees leaned out
over the river, trailing gray moss that moved lazily when a
breeze caught it. Suddenly, a high-pitched screech rose
from the tangled growth along the bank and echoed across
the water.

"What was *that*?" Teddy demanded.

Peregrine shrugged, appearing unconcerned. "A bird
maybe. Or it could be one of the spirits that haunts the
swamps."

Spirits? Beatrice decided not to ask any questions.

Up ahead, she saw what looked like a dam across the
river. There was a wide closed gate in the center, and a
catwalk overhead where two figures stood, watching their
approach.

"We're about to enter the Witches' Sphere," Peregrine
said, his voice squeaking a little with tension. "Let me
handle the border guards."

Beatrice assumed that the guards would be those nasty
smelly trolls that had challenged them on their previous
trip to the Sphere. And she knew how her witch adviser
tended to fall apart when confronted with a troll. But as
the boat glided closer to the catwalk, Beatrice could see
that these guards weren't trolls—in fact, she had no idea

what they were. They stood well over six feet tall and we quite imposing—as one might expect of border guard in the Witches' Sphere—with round hairless heads th gleamed white in the sun like bones in the dessert ar black eyes that glittered in their flat faces. And they we covered from head to toe with what appeared to be lar clam shells. When the boat came to a stop in front of th gate, and the guards stomped heavily down a flight of ste to meet them, their shells rattled and clattered with eve move.

"What *are* they?" Beatrice whispered to Peregrine.

"Shellycoats," Peregrine whispered back. "They haur rivers and streams and are usually in a foul mood. Perfe guards for the waterways."

The two Shellycoats were leaning into the boa staring suspiciously at its occupants.

"State your business," one of the creatures ordered, h deep rattling voice echoing the clatter of his clamshe coat.

Peregrine thrust a sheet of parchment into the guard faces. "I have permission to cross into the Witches' Spher with four witches, two oarsmen, and one cat-familiar he said with authority. Beatrice had learned on their pr vious trip that her timid witch adviser was capable showing surprising strength and courage when circun stances demanded it.

The Shellycoats peered at the document, then back the boat.

"What is *that*?" one of them asked, his voice clinkir and clanking as he pointed at Cyrus.

"That is a witch," Peregrine said tersely.

"I've never seen such a little witch," the Shellycoat boomed. "I think it's a fairy. You aren't authorized to bring a fairy into the Sphere."

Cyrus was visibly cringing from the giant faces looming over him. Peregrine was chewing his lower lip anxiously, obviously racking his brain for a way out of this dilemma. Then all at once the witch adviser drew himself up to his full four-foot height and said coldly, "And you aren't authorized to question official papers signed by the director of the Witches' Institute. Now, if you don't want this little witch to cut you down to his size, I would advise you to let us through. Immediately!"

"And I can do it, too," Cyrus said, regaining his confidence. He scrambled to the top of Beatrice's backpack and glared at the guards.

The Shellycoats exchanged a look. Perhaps Peregrine and Cyrus's threats had a ring of truth because the Shellycoats stepped aside. One of them started to turn a crank beside the gate. Slowly, the gate began to open.

Beatrice glanced back as the boat passed under the catwalk. The Shellycoats were staring after them. Their squinty eyes followed the small craft until it turned a bend in the river.

Peregrine collapsed onto the floor of the boat, muttering that he felt a little faint. Beatrice and Teddy fanned his face with their hats while telling him how brave he was.

"What about me?" Cyrus wanted to know.

"Oh, you're brave, too," Beatrice said with a grin. She waved her hat at him and the breeze sent him flying off the backpack.

"I'll be so glad when this trip is over," Cyrus said wearily.

Peregrine stood up, still a little wobbly, and took his seat beside Ollie. "That's Fools Fire Swamp to our right," Peregrine said.

Feeling tired from the heat, not to mention their encounter with the Shellycoats, Beatrice gave the swamp a perfunctory glance. Then she did a double take. The transparent forms of several ghosts were floating out from behind the trees. The spirits seemed to be gathering along the bank to watch the boat as it passed.

Then Beatrice noticed a woman with a tangle of white hair sitting on a dock with her fishing line in the water. When she saw them, the old woman spread her arms wide as if preparing to conduct an orchestra. Suddenly a great number of fruits and vegetables began to fly out of the swamp and into the little boat. Beatrice and her friends ducked to avoid being struck in the face, but they were soon ankle-deep in fresh produce. The old woman's delighted cackle followed them down the river.

Teddy scowled as she picked pea pods out of her hair. "What was that?" she muttered. "Some weird kind of Welcome Wagon?"

Soon they began to meet other boats. Painted in the brilliant reds and greens and yellows that witches love, the vessels were shaped like dragons and firebirds and large crouching cats. There was even one that looked like a purple goblin sliding through the water on its belly.

"How wonderful!" Beatrice exclaimed.

"Didn't I tell you?" Teddy said happily. "Traditional witches have so much style."

They were still craning their necks and pointing at the amazing watercraft when something about the size of a loaf of bread flew over the side of their boat and landed with a wet *plop* at Cayenne's feet. The startled cat leaped away, hissing and arching her back.

Beatrice thought a fish must have jumped out of the water. She blew her bangs aside and leaned down to investigate. When she saw movement among the brussels sprouts, Beatrice jerked back.

An incredibly ugly head that was mostly eyes suddenly popped up out of the vegetables and peered around. Tiny blunt fingers grabbed hold of Beatrice's backpack and crawled up its side. Cyrus looked a little unnerved when the creature folded its long skinny legs beneath its potbellied body and sat down primly beside him. It was an animal of some sort, most closely resembling a frog with its mottled greenish brown skin and tiny webbed toes. And it was not a pretty sight.

"What *is* it?" Teddy asked, obviously repulsed by the strange little beast.

"This is Longshank, a very good friend of mine," Peregrine said, and Beatrice was startled to see something like a grin plastered across the witch adviser's face. "He's a water leaper, and very good at what he does."

The water leaper's wide mouth spread into what must have been a smile and he poked Peregrine gently with his minuscule fist, as if embarrassed by the praise.

"And exactly what is it that he does?" Beatrice asked.

"Why, he *leaps*," Peregrine said, giving Beatrice a look that clearly said, *You don't know what a water leaper does?*

"Of course he leaps," Ollie murmured, and introduced himself and the others.

When Ollie said Beatrice's name, she smiled at Longshank and said, "Any good friend of Peregrine's is a good friend of mine."

"I've heard all about you," the water leaper said softly. "I wanted to be the first to welcome you."

Beatrice was touched. She looked into Longshank's muddy green eyes and saw only kindness in them. Beatrice reached for his hand and Longshank's cold little fingers quivered against hers.

"Should you ever need my assistance," the water leaper said earnestly, "it would be my honor to serve you."

Peregrine had made his way to the front of the boat and was leaning out across the bow.

"It won't be long now," he said. "Friar's Lantern is just around the bend."

6

Friar's Lantern

They pulled up to a long pier, where a blue dragon boat, a silver cat boat, and a yellow house-boat with turrets like a fairy-tale castle were already docked. While Peregrine helped the others disembark, Cyrus chanted the spell to make himself full-size again. Longshank slipped silently into the water, pausing only long enough to wave good-bye before he vanished.

There was a lot of activity along the waterfront. Beatrice and her friends stood on the wharf swiveling their heads around so as not to miss anything. They watched elves in red caps and polka-dot vests loading kegs marked *Witches' Brew* on the houseboat. A male witch in dark green robes stood on deck directing their efforts. Witches in blue robes were carrying silver nets as delicate as spiders' webs to the dragon boat. Beatrice decided that they must be fishermen. Brownies dressed all in brown—naturally— were unloading crates and barrels from the cat boat and stacking them in a horse-drawn cart. Another cart, pulled by a white goat and driven by a brownie, had already left the wharf and was winding its way up a cobbled road that disappeared over a hill.

Beatrice assumed the road led to Friar's Lantern because she could see a cluster of thatch and gray slate roofs in the distance. She felt a moment of apprehension as she stared at those rooftops. In a short while she would be meeting her mother's aunts, who could probably answer all her questions about Nina Bailey's past. Of course, Beatrice wanted to know—she *had* to know!—but that didn't keep her from worrying about what the answers might be.

As Beatrice turned back to the pier, where Peregrine and Ollie were unloading their backpacks from the boat, a small boy standing at the edge of the wharf caught her eye. Actually, it wasn't the boy that captured her attention so much as the large orange cat he was dangling over the water. It appeared that the child meant to drop the cat into the river!

The boy looked to be seven or eight—certainly old enough to know better, Beatrice fumed. She dropped her hat and jacket on the wharf and started toward him. But just as she came close enough to call out to him, the cat started to hiss and struggle to be set free.

"Stop that!" the boy demanded, his face screwed up in frustration. Then he let out a cry of pain.

Beatrice saw a trickle of blood on the boy's arm just as the cat fell from his hands. An instant later, there was a splash when the animal hit the water.

Horrified, Beatrice yelled at the boy, "How could you be so cruel? He'll drown!"

His eyes a startled blue under uncombed sandy hair, the boy said quickly, "I didn't mean—" Then he stopped, and the shock in his face changed to surliness. "The old flea-bit thing hurt me. You think I care if he drowns?"

But there wasn't time for arguments. Beatrice ran to the edge of the wharf and spotted the cat floundering to stay afloat. She pulled off her shoes and was poised to dive in when a strong hand grabbed her arm.

"Stand back," a male voice said.

Beatrice's head jerked up, and she had a fleeting glimpse of a man's face before he dove off the wharf into the water. Everyone gathered to watch as the man swam toward the cat. Beatrice held her breath until she saw him reach out and grab the animal firmly around the middle. Apparently too exhausted to put up a fight, the cat went limp. Onlookers cheered when the man started swimming back with the cat in tow.

Beatrice crouched down and extended her hand, intending to help pull them ashore. But when the cat's rescuer reached the wharf, he flew out of the water and landed next to Beatrice. After gently placing the cat into her arms, he began to wring water out of his dark red robes.

Beatrice found her jacket and wrapped it around the terrified cat, studying the man out of the corner of her eye.

He was young—*No more than eighteen*, Beatrice thought—and very good-looking. He had a lean face with pronounced cheekbones and dark velvety eyes. His hair was black and was already beginning to form wet curls across his forehead.

Then Beatrice realized that the man was watching her, as well. "Thank you," she said, feeling herself blush.

His eyes twinkled when he smiled. "I was happy to do it," he replied, and glancing at the cat, added, "This guy's an old friend of mine. By the way, I'm Fillian Hawthorn."

"Beatrice Bailiwick."

He nodded, still smiling. "I know. We've all been waiting for you to get here."

Unsure how to respond to that, Beatrice turned to the boy, who was scowling at her. "As for you—"

"Yeah, yeah, yeah," he interrupted in a sassy voice. "I'm a very bad boy. Don't waste your breath, sister. I've heard it all before."

Beatrice felt her pulse quicken with anger. *What a nasty child!* "Look here—" she started.

But the boy cut her off again. "No, *you* look here. You're new to Friar's Lantern, so you don't know about me. Just take my word for it—I'm *big* trouble."

Fillian was regarding the boy with a bemused expression. "This impudent wild child is named Bing," he told Beatrice. "And his bark is really worse than his bite."

A nearby fisherman had been listening. "You can't convince me of that," he said, and gave Bing a hard knowing look. "From what I've seen, he *is* big trouble."

The boy smirked, apparently pleased by the fisherman's assessment.

Fillian frowned at Bing. "There's no excuse for being cruel to an innocent cat," he said.

A look of protest flashed across Bing's face. "Innocent! Do you see where he scratched me? And, anyhow, I wasn't going to—"

Fillian held up his hands to silence the boy. "If I ever hear of you mistreating another animal, I'll tell Miss

Primrose about this," he said. "You know how mad she'll be if she finds out that you nearly drowned her cat, intentional or not."

"Did you say *Primrose?*" Beatrice asked.

Fillian's smile returned. "That's right. Primrose Merriwether, your great-aunt. And *that*," he said, pointing to the orange cat now purring in Beatrice's arms, "is Miss Primrose's cat Lysander."

Teddy had come to stand with Beatrice and was giving her significant looks.

"Oh—" Beatrice said, realizing that she had forgotten all about Teddy and the others. "I want you to meet my friends."

As Beatrice introduced them, Peregrine ducked his head, Cyrus grinned, Teddy started firing questions at Fillian about his life in the Witches' Sphere, and Cayenne gazed at him intently before curling up in Beatrice's hat to take a much-needed nap. Only Ollie responded in a way that surprised Beatrice. Ollie, who was nearly always a gentleman, nodded curtly and then turned to stare out over the water.

"So did you grow up in Friar's Lantern?" Teddy was asking Fillian.

"No, I haven't been here long," he replied. "I'm in the Witches' Service Corps and this is my first-year assignment."

"Then you're Classical." Teddy's tone changed to one of near awe. "Is it two years you have to serve? You're supposed to help out with natural disasters, aren't you? Have there been any since you got here?"

"How about giving him time to answer?" Beatrice cut in.

Fillian's laugh was good-natured. "That's okay, I don't mind Teddy's questions." And then to Teddy, he said, "Yes, it's two years, and yes, we respond to natural—as well as *unnatural*—disasters when they occur. But most of the time we visit witches who need the company and a little help. I read to them, write letters, shop for groceries—that sort of thing."

Teddy's eyes glowed as she hung on to his every word. Beatrice could almost hear what her friend was thinking: *He's handsome and smart—and Classical. Well dressed and brave—and Classical. Charming and interesting and—let us not forget—Classical!*

Oh, brother, Beatrice thought. "We should probably go find my great-aunts, don't you think?" she suggested, giving Teddy a nudge.

"Good idea," Fillian said. "I'll be glad to take you. They're at work this time of day. Miss Primrose owns a restaurant and Miss Laurel has a little hat shop next door. Bing," he added, "you can help carry their bags."

"*Right*," the boy said sarcastically. "I'm out of here." He glared at Beatrice one last time and started running toward the swamp.

Beatrice watched him disappear into the trees. "I hope I don't meet up with that little monster again," she muttered.

"It's likely that you will," Fillian said pleasantly. "He lives at Merriwether House with Miss Primrose and Miss Laurel."

Beatrice's face fell. "I'm sorry to hear that," she replied.

Fillian laughed. Then he said, "Well, let's get going, shall we? I know you must all be tired after your trip."

"Not especially," Ollie answered brusquely.

Beatrice looked at Ollie and saw that he didn't appear happy. Neither did Peregrine.

"I'm sure you have witches to visit," Peregrine said to Fillian in a surprisingly forceful voice. "I can see that they reach their destination."

"Actually, I was going that way," Fillian replied, heaving Beatrice's backpack to his shoulder.

Peregrine gave a huge sigh. He was apparently feeling dejected because it seemed that Fillian was trying to take over his job. As for Ollie . . . Beatrice pondered his disgruntled expression with bewilderment. She didn't have a clue.

Lysander seemed fully recovered and was struggling to get out of Beatrice's arms. She placed the cat on the ground. Awake from her nap, Cayenne stood and stretched, then sidled over to meet the orange cat. The felines touched noses and sniffed before setting off together down the cobbled road.

Beatrice and the others followed. As they walked up the hill, Beatrice noticed a weathered sign that read *Will-o'-the-wisp Road*. This reminded her of the strange lights—sometimes called will-o'-the-wisp, her great-aunt had said—that moved through the marshes at night. Beatrice glanced back at the swamps that spread out in all directions from the river. They were dark and eerie, even in daylight. Beatrice wondered with a sense of foreboding if they would have to travel through swamps to reach Werewolf Close.

"The village is just over this hill," Fillian said.

"And Werewolf Close?" Beatrice asked. "Where is that from here?"

Fillian stopped and turned toward the wharf. "On the other side of the river," he said, pointing, "and through the swamp about two miles."

Beatrice's heart sank. The others stared solemnly across the water at the dense growth of moss-draped trees on the other side.

"We'll need a boat," Cyrus said in a small voice.

"That should be easy enough to get around here," Teddy assured him.

"Finding a boat is the least of our problems," Ollie spoke up, sounding uncharacteristically cross.

"You're right about that," Fillian said darkly.

He turned back to the road and resumed walking. The others fell into step beside him, thoroughly subdued.

"I think you'll like Friar's Lantern," Fillian told them, sounding suddenly cheerful again. "The Department of Tourism touts it as 'a delightfully picturesque village that shouldn't be missed.'"

A few minutes later, Beatrice and her friends saw for themselves what the Department of Tourism was talking about. Quaint shops of faded brick and old stone faced each other across Will-o'-the-wisp Road. Small whitewashed cottages with thatched roofs were interspersed among the businesses, their gardens lush with greenery and colorful flowers.

And everywhere Beatrice looked witches were briskly going about their lives: sweeping doorsteps and watering flowers, haggling with merchants at outdoor produce stands, unloading carts and rolling barrels into shops, and calling out greetings to their friends and neighbors.

They had walked about a block, passing a post office and shops that sold everything from magic crystals to designer witches' robes, when Fillian came to a stop in front of a large arched opening. A stone sign above the arch read *Cattail Court*.

"This way," Fillian said.

They followed him through the opening and found themselves in a bricked courtyard with shops on either side. At the far end was a large white building with chairs and tables arranged out front under blue umbrellas. The sign over the door showed a handsome orange cat against a blue background. The cat was playing a fiddle and seemed to be dancing on a carpet of silver stars.

"That's The Cat and the Fiddle," Fillian said, "Miss Primrose's restaurant. Guess who posed for the sign," he added, grinning.

As they headed toward the restaurant, Beatrice noticed shops called Maiden's Blush and Beyond Thyme. There was a pub named The Muddy Duck. And then there were the cats. They were sitting on rooftops and doorsteps, reclining on tree limbs, and curled up in flowerpots. Beatrice could see how the courtyard had acquired its name, since there were at least two dozen cattails here of every style and color.

Teddy had a big smile on her face. "This is great!" she exclaimed. "I *knew* I was going to love a Traditional witch village."

About that time, Beatrice noticed a female witch crouching on the roof of the restaurant. She was wearing orange robes and a big straw hat that shaded her face, but Beatrice could see spikes of pale red hair poking out through the straw. The witch had a heavy tool belt around her waist, and was hammering on the roof with such fervor that her intent seemed more to destroy than to repair.

Beatrice was taken aback. She stared up at the woman for a moment, then looked quizzically at Fillian.

He smiled and nodded. "Yes, that's her. Miss Primrose Merriwether, your great-aunt."

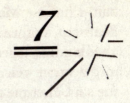

7

Banished!

People were peering through windows and doorways, and even coming out of their shops, to stare at the new arrivals. They made no attempt to conceal their curiosity.

Primrose saw Beatrice's group and waved. "I'll be right here," she called out loudly. The next thing Beatrice knew, her great-aunt was sailing down from the roof and landing with a gentle thud on the courtyard bricks.

Teddy leaned close to Beatrice and said, "Did you see that? She flew like Fillian did. We can learn a lot from these witches."

Primrose took a step toward them and her tool belt dropped down around her ankles. She tripped over it and fell flat.

Her eyes sparkling with merriment, Beatrice whispered to Teddy, "I already know how to do *that*."

Primrose scrambled to her feet and kicked the tool belt aside with a growl. Her face looked freshly scrubbed and shining, the dusting of freckles across her nose giving the illusion of youth. Except for the fan of wrinkles around her bright blue eyes and faded streaks through her red hair, Primrose Merriwether didn't look much older than Beatrice's mother.

Primrose loped over to Beatrice, her mouth stretched into a warm welcoming smile. "You have to be Beatrice," she said. "Let me take a good look at you."

Primrose's eyes moved from Beatrice's face to her feet and back again. "I would have known you anywhere," she said with a nod of satisfaction. "That hair . . . the Merriwether nose . . . And you have my mother's hands—long fingers, you know."

"Hello, Aunt Primrose," Beatrice said. "Thank you for inviting us to stay with you. These are my friends."

Introductions were made and Primrose beamed at them all. Then she hugged Beatrice and said, "I'm so happy you're here, I might cry."

"Miss Primrose, I thought you were too tough for that," Fillian said, teasing her gently.

"I'm tough enough to handle the likes of you," Primrose said sassily, but the look she gave Fillian was affectionate. "Can you stay for lunch? The special is crab and rat tail pie, your favorite."

"I wish I could." The regret in Fillian's voice sounded genuine. "But I have to look in on Yorick Figlock."

"I don't envy you," Primrose said bluntly. "That witch is off his rocker."

"Now, Miss Primrose."

"Well, he is," she declared. "Last week Juliana Bright took him some books from the library and he was telling her that he saw a vampire coming out of the swamp." Primrose snorted. "Everybody knows there hasn't been a

74

vampire in this part of the Sphere for fifty years. And you've heard the rumors—"

"I've heard them," Fillian said quickly. "But they can't be true."

Primrose realized that Beatrice and her friends were waiting politely for the conversation to be over, not knowing *what* they were talking about. "We're being rude discussing things you children know nothing about," she said. "Yorick Figlock is this crazy old witch—" She caught Fillian's grimace and grinned. "A *crazy* old witch," she repeated wickedly. "Anyway, Yorick was always odd but still had his faculties—then last year, he just up and disappeared. When he came back a few weeks later, he looked bad, let me tell you. He was all scarred and limping—and crazy as they come!"

"Miss *Primrose*," Fillian said sternly.

Primrose went on like he hadn't said a word. "Some people say Yorick was in Werewolf Close all that time, and that he barely escaped with his life."

"Tell me how he could have escaped at all," Fillian said reasonably. "Or gotten in, for that matter. *No one* can make it through the fog and past the werewolves."

Now Beatrice and her friends were listening with rapt attention. *We need to talk to this crazy witch*, Beatrice thought.

Suddenly Primrose looked down and saw her wet cat sitting next to Cayenne. Then her gaze shifted to Fillian, who was also soaking wet.

Primrose's eyes narrowed. "What happened to the two of you?" she demanded.

Fillian shrugged, grinning, and said nothing.

Primrose frowned and leaned down to pick up Lysander. "Come on, you rascal," she scolded, scratching him under the chin. "There's dragon's milk waiting for you inside." Primrose looked at Beatrice and cocked her head at Cayenne. "Is this lovely girl yours?"

Beatrice nodded. "That's Cayenne."

"Well, come on, Cayenne," Primrose said. "We'll get some dragon's milk for you, too. And the rest of you have a treat in store. I serve up the best food in the Witches' Sphere!"

"I really have to go," Fillian said, and turning to Beatrice, added, "but I'll see you soon. I'm always stopping in at The Cat and the Fiddle."

"Thanks for bringing us here," Beatrice said. She glanced at the orange cat in Primrose's arms. "And—everything."

Fillian nodded. "Sure thing. I'll catch you later."

They were headed for the restaurant when Beatrice heard a woman's voice calling, "Prim! *Primrose Merriwether!* You were supposed to tell me when Beatrice got here."

Beatrice and her friends saw a woman coming out of the shop next to The Cat and the Fiddle. The sign over the door read *Head in the Clouds.* In smaller print were the words *Fine Hats for the Discriminating Witch.*

"I figured you'd be watching, Laurel, like everybody else," Primrose answered impatiently. She looked around with disgust at all the people who had gathered to catch a glimpse of Beatrice.

Laurel Merriwether's lips had formed the perfect pout. To Beatrice, it seemed that everything about this stunning witch was perfect. She was tall and slender, and somehow managed to look graceful even as she elbowed her way through the crowd of gawkers. Laurel's black hair fell softly to her shoulders, the gray at the temples appearing perfectly placed. Her large blue-gray eyes matched her smoke-colored silk robes, and her robes matched the blue-gray cat that walked regally beside her. Beatrice glanced at Primrose, who had a smudge of dirt on her nose and a hole in her hat where the straw had started to unravel, and wondered if Laurel might not be adopted.

"Hello, sweetheart," Laurel said, swooping down on Beatrice and embracing her. "I'm sorry I wasn't here to meet you." She shot Primrose a look, then smiled at Beatrice. A dimple appeared at the corner of her mouth.

"That's all right, Aunt Laurel," Beatrice said quickly. She didn't want to be the cause of a family feud, but something told her that bickering was probably normal for the Merriwethers.

"Anyway, we can still have lunch together." Laurel cast a smug glance at her sister. "Primrose has to work during lunch, so we'll have time to get to know one another."

"I won't be working *all* the time," Primrose informed her sister, "so don't think you'll have Beatrice entirely to yourself."

"You've already had time with her," Laurel said crossly. "She's my great-niece, too, you know."

While the sisters squabbled, Teddy said softly to Beatrice, "Your Aunt Laurel is gorgeous. Do you think she'd help me with my wardrobe?"

Beatrice was watching the way Laurel straightened her robes so that they fell perfectly to her small slippered feet.

77

"I imagine," Beatrice said wryly, "that nothing would please Aunt Laurel more."

Peregrine was glancing anxiously at the watch on his skinny wrist. "It's time for me to leave," he said to Beatrice. "Actually, past time. Primrose knows how to reach me at the Witches' Institute if you need me."

Beatrice had learned from their last trip to the Sphere that it was Peregrine's job to deliver them to their destination, and then they didn't see him again until all the tough stuff was over. She was still wondering how he had earned the title *Witch Adviser*, since he didn't seem to offer much advice.

"You'll be receiving word from the Witches' Executive Committee on how to proceed," Peregrine went on. "Just enjoy yourselves until the letter arrives. And *remember*," he added solemnly, "Dally Rumpe can take any shape he wants, so be cautious with people you don't know."

Which is basically everyone, Beatrice thought. She nodded and thanked Peregrine for bringing them to the Sphere safely.

"I'm sure someone else could have done just as well," Peregrine said, his voice taking on an injured tone. "Fillian Hawthorn, for instance."

So Peregrine was still hurt that Fillian had stepped on his turf. "I wouldn't *want* anyone else to accompany us to the Sphere," Beatrice said gently, and was pleased to see a little smile tug at Peregrine's lips.

"And the boat worked out fine," she assured him. But Peregrine had already vanished.

"Let's get inside out of this heat," Primrose was saying. "A glass of cat's purr tea should do the trick."

Beatrice turned to follow the others into the restaurant and nearly tripped over a small man in a brown cap and tunic. He had shaggy brown hair and a scraggly beard, and was peering up at Beatrice with bold black eyes in a way that seemed both impolite and threatening. Had he been more than three feet tall, he might have frightened Beatrice.

Primrose looked back and stopped in her tracks when she saw the little man. "What is it you want, Nobby Chinwhisker?" she asked sharply.

"I came to introduce myself," Nobby answered slyly. "Is this *her* daughter?"

Laurel was regarding Nobby with an expression of distaste. "This is Beatrice," she said, sliding an arm around Beatrice's shoulder.

Beatrice recognized that Nobby Chinwhisker was a brownie, and a rude one at that, referring to Beatrice's mother as *her* in that offensive way.

The brownie was still staring at her, his little black eyes glinting like chips of onyx. "I'm Nobby Chinwhisker," he said, puffing out his chest. "I own The Muddy Duck."

He pointed to the pub, where a sign by the door featured a crude painting that closely resembled a brown chicken. Beneath the sign stood a fat brown creature that looked like . . . Yes, it was definitely a pig.

"That's Valentina," Nobby said with pride. "The best mouser in the Sphere. She's won ribbons for it and everything."

"How nice," Beatrice said faintly, and moved around him toward the door to the restaurant. But his next words made Beatrice freeze in her tracks.

"Are you going to stay now that you're here?" Nobby asked, a hint of malevolence in his voice. "Or do you take after your mother?"

"That's it!" Primrose exploded. "Get out of here, you odious little brownie. Shoo, shoo," she said, making sweeping motions with her hands.

"Cool your cauldrons, Primmy," Nobby said lazily. Then he remarked with a smirk, "Witches are so emotional."

"I'll show you emotional!" Primrose shouted, looking like she might start pounding him with her hammer.

"Primrose, don't make a scene," Laurel said delicately.

Primrose glared at her and then at the snickering Nobby. She took Beatrice by the shoulders and pointed her toward the restaurant, then started herding them all through the doorway.

Once inside, Laurel patted Beatrice on the arm and said, "Just ignore what Nobby Chinwhisker has to say. I mean, who can take a man with a pig seriously?"

"But he was so nasty," Beatrice said, realizing that she was trembling. "Did you notice how he called my mother *her*? He could have at least used her name."

"No he couldn't," Laurel said.

Beatrice looked up, startled. "What do you mean?"

"Your mother was banished from the Witches' Sphere," Laurel replied sadly. "No one's allowed to speak the name of a Begone."

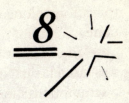

Cattail Court

Beatrice felt a rush of anguish. Her mother had been banished! What terrible thing could she have done to deserve that?

Primrose shot her sister an irritated look. "Now isn't the time," she hissed. "Say no more about it!"

But Beatrice had questions, a *lot* of questions. "What's a Begone?" she asked Laurel.

Laurel cut her eyes at Primrose, then said to Beatrice, "A Begone is a witch who's been banished from the Sphere for breaking the rules. The banishment is forever and can never be lifted."

"Laurel, can't you find something else to talk about?" Primrose snapped. "I've seen you go on for hours about whether to use velvet or chenille for one of your hats. Bore us with some hat talk."

"No," Beatrice said quickly. "I want to know why my mother was banished."

Primrose glanced around to see if anyone was listening. "We'll talk later," she said in a low voice. "This isn't something we can discuss—publicly."

Beatrice sighed. She supposed she would have to accept Primrose's decision for now, but she didn't intend to wait very long. She had to know what her mother had done.

"You all must be starved," Primrose said in a voice that was just a little too hearty. "Go wash up and we'll bring you a scrumptious lunch."

When Laurel led Beatrice and her friends through the dining room, Beatrice noticed that most of the tables were filled. Witches looked up with obvious interest as Beatrice walked by.

The ladies' room was amazing. Vines covered the ceiling, creating a canopy of leaves and white flowers overhead. The walls were draped with soft green moss, and garden benches had been arranged under arbors that were covered with pink roses. Seated on one of the benches was a tiny woman with golden hair spilling over the shoulders of her white gown and falling in silky waves to her bare feet.

When Beatrice and Teddy asked about washing their hands, the woman poured water from a silver pitcher and filled their palms with creamy rose-scented soap.

"Are you a fairy?" Beatrice guessed.

The woman looked mildly offended. "I should say not," she replied. "I'm a river nymph. My name is Trill."

"I've never met a river nymph before," Teddy said, admiring the tiny necklace of shells and pearls around Trill's neck.

Trill yawned, seeming bored and out of sorts. "I should be at the river right now," she said crossly, "singing my heart out. That's what river nymphs do, in case you didn't know."

"So what are you doing here?" Teddy asked.

Trill handed them towels. "I'm working," the river nymph said curtly. "You know—to put food on the table? And my shift isn't over for another hour."

When Beatrice and Teddy emerged from the ladies' room, two female elves introduced themselves as Puddifoot and Glee. The very blond and very perky elves led them to a table by the window where Laurel, Ollie, Cyrus, and Cayenne were already seated. Laurel's blue-gray cat lay on her mistress' shoulder.

"This is Grayshadows,'' Laurel said, reaching up to stroke the cat's silky fur.

"She's gorgeous," Teddy said. "The perfect cat for you."

"I know," Laurel said simply.

Cyrus looked down at his menu and murmured, "I was afraid of this."

"He doesn't like witch food," Teddy explained to Laurel, then gave Cyrus a withering look.

Ollie's eyes drifted down his menu. "Glowworm gumbo, lizard gizzards, red beans and crickets . . . Cyrus, it all sounds really good."

"I suggest that we start with leek and bat-claw soup," Laurel said, "and you have to try the steamed moths and crawfish. We have a new chef, and she has a way with moths."

Beatrice caught Cyrus's dubious expression. "They serve hexburgers and fury fries, too," she told him.

Cyrus looked relieved. "Now you're talking."

While they were waiting to be served, Beatrice glanced around at the other diners. She noticed a dark-haired man sitting with a blond woman at a nearby table. The woman was very pretty.

"That's Makepeace Drummond," Laurel said, following Beatrice's eyes. "He teaches Witch History and The Healing Arts at the witch academy. The woman is his wife, Skye." Laurel regarded them thoughtfully. "They're nice witches, for the most part, although Skye can act superior at times."

Beatrice noticed the edge in Laurel's voice and wondered if it might not come from rivalry between two beautiful witches. "And the cat?" Beatrice asked, referring to the small black feline napping beside Skye Drummond's plate.

"Piccolo," Laurel said. "Also superior."

Beatrice realized that Skye Drummond was staring at her. Beatrice dropped her eyes and concentrated on smoothing the napkin in her lap. She thought she had detected something less than friendly in the blond witch's face.

Puddifoot and Glee had just brought their food when a tall thin man with frizzy salt-and-pepper hair stomped into the restaurant. As he rushed past Beatrice's table, he left behind the strong scent of herbs. Stalking behind him was a grizzled gray striped cat.

The man marched purposefully to the Drummonds' table and began shouting in an angry voice. Skye Drummond's pretty face turned red and she started yelling in response. Soon Primrose had joined them and was trying to get them to quiet down.

"That's Magnus Pinch," Laurel said without much interest. "Magnus owns the herb shop, Beyond Thyme. Skye has a cosmetics shop and beauty parlor called Maiden's Blush."

The angry voices had risen an octave, with Primrose now screaming for them to calm down. Ollie had to practically shout to ask, "What are they fighting about?"

"Magnus is always accusing Skye of stealing his secret herbal formulas for her line of beauty products," Laurel said. "Of course, Skye denies it. Have you tried the spider's web tea?" she asked, looking around the table. "It's so refreshing."

Skye had now leaped up from the table and was jabbing her finger into Magnus's arm while she continued to scream at him. Then he was pounding his fist in the air for emphasis while shouting at her. Makepeace Drummond glanced up at them and then went back to eating his lunch.

Suddenly Beatrice felt a tremor. Then the building started to shake, the vibrations causing plates and glasses to fall off the tables and crash to the floor.

"What's happening?" Teddy yelled. "An earthquake?"

"Of course not," Laurel yelled back. "It's just angry vibes."

Now Primrose was pushing Skye and Magnus toward the door. "That's it!" she screeched. "You've broken the last dish you're going to break in *my* restaurant."

When the two had been shoved outside, the noise level died down considerably and the building settled back on its foundation with a groan. Beatrice was able to ask in a nearly normal voice as she stared at the broken crockery on the floor, "You mean this was all caused by their anger?"

"That's right," Laurel answered. "When witches get mad, their angry energy is quite powerful. One time," she added, giggling as she remembered, "Magnus was so furious with Skye, he caused a keg of witches' brew to split wide open. It poured down on Primrose's head."

Everyone around the table was grinning at a mental image of how Primrose might have responded to that.

"Normally, we get along well in the court," Laurel went on. "But Magnus is very secretive about his formulas—and everything else, for that matter. We don't know *what* he's concocting in that shop of his, but whatever it is, he guards it closely. And when he thinks another witch is stepping into his territory, *the fur can fly*."

They all watched out the window as the battle raged on in the courtyard. Now the cats had gotten in on the act. While Skye and Magnus continued to scream and point fingers, their cats began to circle each other, arching their backs and hissing. Then Lysander dashed out of the restaurant to join the fray. Cayenne made a move to follow him, but Beatrice grabbed her.

"Don't even think about it," Beatrice said.

Grayshadows narrowed her eyes as the cats outside began yowling and spitting, and then looked away with disdain.

Beatrice grinned, thinking that the blue-gray cat was every bit as beautiful and vain as her mistress. *Of course* she wouldn't stoop to scrapping and screeching with the common cats.

When Beatrice looked out again, at least fifteen cats had entered the fight. And the fur was flying.

Beatrice was just finishing her soup when Primrose came to the table to introduce her chef, a girl named Molly Wilder.

Molly was bright-eyed and attractive—*and young,* Beatrice thought, deciding that she couldn't be much older than Beatrice herself. The girl's dark hair was pulled up into two short ponytails that made her appear younger than she probably was, and her smile was friendly.

"I've collected all the newspaper and magazine articles about you guys," Molly said. "What you did in Winter Wood was spectacular."

Teddy was obviously delighted by the girl's frank admiration, and Cyrus and Ollie seemed pleased. Beatrice was simply embarrassed.

Anxious to change the subject, Beatrice said, "You're awfully young to be such an accomplished chef. This meal is wonderful."

Molly's face lit up. "I've always loved to cook," she said, "and I couldn't believe it when Miss Primrose agreed to give me a chance."

"Hiring you was the smartest thing I ever did," Primrose declared. "People come all the way from Sticky Wicket and Shufflebottom for your gumbo. If I don't watch out, you're going to make me a rich witch."

"My parents died in an accident," Molly explained to Beatrice and her friends, "and I didn't know what I was going to do. Then Miss Primrose and Miss Laurel let me come live with them, and Miss Prim gave me a job here, and—" Molly spread out her hands and smiled, "my life has been great ever since."

"So you live with my great-aunts, too?" Beatrice asked.

Molly grinned at her. "That 'too' tells me that you've already met Bing. *I knew it!*" she exclaimed, seeing the subtle change in Beatrice's expression. "He doesn't always put his best foot forward when he meets new people. But don't worry—part of my job is taking care of him. I'll make sure he doesn't put a snake in your bed like he did to me once."

Teddy's eyebrows shot up. "A *snake?*"

Molly laughed. "Bing's not a bad kid. Really. He's just a troubled little witch."

After Molly and Primrose were gone, Teddy said, "A troubled little witch, huh? I'd better not find any reptiles in my bed, or he'll find out the *meaning* of troubled."

"I *told* Prim not to take him in," Laurel said vaguely. "First Molly, then Bing. You'd think we were running a halfway house or something."

About that time, Skye marched back into the restaurant with a puffed-out Piccolo in her arms. Skye's face was flushed and her blond hair was pointing in all directions. She sat down heavily across from her husband and said loud enough for Beatrice to hear, "Why would I need to steal his formulas? I'm not even sure he *has* any formulas! If I were still casting spells, I'd turn him into a rutabaga."

Makepeace Drummond listened until she was finished and then went back to eating. "This crab and rat tail pie is excellent," he said.

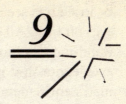

The House on Muttering Lane

"I'll take you home and let you get settled," Laurel said to Beatrice and her friends. "Prim can't leave till later."

They were gathering up their belongings when the door opened and a young man entered the restaurant. He was wearing faded blue robes of a rough weave that were frayed at the cuffs and hem. His face was so deeply tanned it was nearly the same leathery brown as his thick unkempt hair and heavy eyebrows. He looked around the room with his eyes narrowed and his square chin jutting out as if he were expecting trouble. *Or hoping for it*, Beatrice thought.

Everyone in the restaurant became quiet when the man swaggered into the room. They watched him out of the corner of their eyes, and disapproval settled over their faces. It was obvious that this witch wasn't popular with the locals.

He walked over to a table in the corner and sat down, tipping his chair back and stretching out his long legs in an arrogant way. He was so different from anyone else

Beatrice had seen in Friar's Lantern, she couldn't take her eyes off him. All at once he seemed to notice that she was watching him and he fixed his piercing gaze on her, his eyes expressing more of a challenge than curiosity. The man's entire demeanor was one of sullen defiance.

Beatrice felt the color rising in her face. She looked away, then back again. He was still staring at her.

"Who is *that*?" Teddy asked, gaping at the man as she stuffed her jacket into her backpack. "All he needs is a motorcycle and a tattoo."

"Don't look at him," Laurel said in a low voice. "That's what he wants—everybody's attention."

"Well, he's got it," Beatrice said.

Then she saw Primrose going over to the man's table. *Was she going to kick him out?* Beatrice wondered. Having seen her Aunt Primrose in action, that wouldn't have surprised her, only this guy looked a lot tougher than Nobby Chinwhisker and Magnus Pinch. But astonishingly, Primrose was grinning at the man. Now she was talking to him in what seemed to be a friendly manner. And he—well, he wasn't exactly smiling, but his expression had softened, and he was looking at Primrose in a way that was almost warm.

In the glacial silence that filled the room, Beatrice heard Primrose say, "Will you have the usual, Xan, or do you want to live dangerously and try something different?" There was laughter in her voice, and this time he actually smiled.

It was more of a grimace, actually, but Beatrice thought it was meant to be a smile. Then the man—this Xan—said something, but it came out as a low rumble and Beatrice couldn't understand the words.

"Well, let's get moving," Laurel said briskly. "I need to get back to the shop."

As Beatrice followed the others out the door, she glanced at Xan. He was staring at her again, the softness in his face replaced by something hard and pitiless—and disturbingly personal, it seemed to Beatrice.

"All right, Miss Laurel," Teddy said after they left the restaurant, "tell us about that guy. What's his name and what prison has he been in?"

"He's the shame of the village, that's what he is," Laurel said, appearing agitated. "His name is Xan Renshaw, and none of you—" She paused for emphasis as she looked into each of their faces, "—should have anything to do with him."

"Aunt Primrose seems to like him," Beatrice remarked.

Laurel rolled her eyes. "That's my sister for you, always looking for some underdog to champion. Next she'll be having *him* move in." Laurel was leading them around the side of the restaurant. "Prim won't hear anything bad about him—but the whole village knows he's dangerous."

"Dangerous *how?*" Teddy demanded.

They had come to a wooden gate set into a brick wall. Laurel reached to open the door, then turned around. She glanced back at the restaurant to make sure there was no one nearby. "He's a *smuggler*," she said in a stage whisper. "He lives across the river in the *swamp* with all the other ne'er-do-wells."

Beatrice's heart began to beat faster. *Werewolf Close* was across the river.

"What does he smuggle?" Cyrus asked in the same loud whisper.

"Well, they *say*," Laurel replied, a hint of excitement creeping into her voice, "that he smuggles in exotic poisons and deadly herbs that aren't easy to come by in this part of the Sphere—for witches who practice the dark arts."

"*Whoa!*" Ollie exclaimed. "Are there practitioners of the dark arts in Friar's Lantern?"

"I don't *think* so," Laurel said tentatively. "We have mostly good magic here. But renegade witches have always hidden out in the swamps, encouraged by Dally Rumpe, of course. He protects the likes of Xan Renshaw—so don't go wandering around outside the village," she warned, "*especially* after dark."

Laurel opened the gate in the wall and they followed her onto a pretty street that was lined with charming cottages. But Beatrice was absorbed in her own thoughts and barely noticed her surroundings.

"Aunt Laurel, do you think Yorick Figlock really managed to get inside Werewolf Close?" Beatrice asked.

"The rumors started when he disappeared because he had family in the Close and was obsessed with getting them out. But as for whether he actually made it in . . ." Laurel's voice trailed off and she shrugged. "Personally, I think Yorick was just lost in the swamp all that time. He sure looked and smelled like it when he came back."

Across the street was a moss green cottage surrounded by flowering trees. "That's Merriwether House," Laurel said. A shower of white blossoms rained down on them as they walked up the stone walk to the front porch.

"So why does Aunt Primrose like Xan?" Beatrice persisted.

"Because she's out of her mind," Laurel declared. "Nobody in the village will have anything to do with him, so Prim feels sorry for him. He comes in for most of his meals and runs off the other customers, but will Primrose see the truth? *Nooooo.* In her mind, he's just another lost sheep. More like a wolf that's *after* the sheep, I'd say."

The front door was painted bright pink. Even Beatrice surfaced from her musings to notice that. Then Laurel led them inside and they stepped into an entry hall that seemed to glow, as if the walls had been painted with sunshine. Through an arched doorway on one side of the hall, Beatrice saw a room filled with overstuffed chairs, a plump sofa, and lots of bookshelves. On the other side of the hall was the dining room. There were paintings on all the walls—a few landscapes, but mostly portraits of witches.

Laurel noticed Beatrice looking at a painting of a red-haired woman with twinkling eyes and several cowlicks.

"That's Prim's and my mother," Laurel said, gazing at the picture with obvious affection. "Isadora Bobo Merriwether. She was famous for curing boils and ear mites. Very talented."

Then Laurel moved to the next portrait. Beatrice followed her and stared into the face of a heavy-jowled man whose eyes appeared to be crossed.

"That's our grandfather, Dogmael Merriwether," Laurel said with considerably less fondness. "He had no talent at all—unless you count being able to turn cheese green."

"And over here," Laurel said, indicating a portrait of a grim old man wearing a black pointed hat, "is our great-grandfather Anskar Merriwether. He discovered the meaning of life."

Beatrice was impressed. "What *is* the meaning of life."

Laurel frowned. "You know, I don't think anybody ever asked him," she replied vaguely. And as if it didn't matter much, anyway, she said with sudden energy, "Well, come along, and I'll take you to your rooms."

Laurel led them up a steep staircase and down a hall past two closed doors. "Molly and Bing's rooms," Laurel said. Then she stopped in front of a third door. "Beatrice, you and Teddy will be in here," she said, "and Ollie and Cyrus are across the hall. Your bath is next door to the girls' room."

Beatrice and Teddy walked into a room with willow green walls and wood floors that gleamed in the afternoon sunlight. There was a heavy carved dresser and twin four-poster beds covered with plump white comforters. Cayenne leaped onto one of the beds and sank up to her elbows.

"Feather mattresses," Laurel explained.

"It's very pretty," Beatrice said, looking around at the framed herbal prints on the walls. And then she noticed the photograph. Beatrice felt a shock of recognition when her eyes fell on a framed photo on one of the bedside tables. Looking back at her from inside the tarnished silver frame were three smiling girls with their arms around one another. But it was the girl in the middle who held Beatrice's attention. She had a thin angular face and pale red hair cut straight across at the shoulder. It was a picture of Beatrice's mother.

Beatrice walked over and picked up the photograph. Her eyes slid to the other girls. The blonde looked familiar . . . and suddenly Beatrice realized that this was a younger version of Skye Drummond. And the other girl—Beatrice breathed in sharply—the girl with dark auburn hair was Aura Featherstone!

Laurel went to stand beside Beatrice and slipped an arm around her great-niece's waist. "I forgot that was in here," Laurel said softly. "This was your mother's room when she lived with us."

"When was that?" Beatrice asked, not taking her eyes off the photo.

Laurel sighed, as if the memory were painful. "She came to visit when she was sixteen and decided to stay. She left two years later."

Beatrice sat down heavily on the bed, sinking into the feather mattress. Cayenne crawled into her lap and Beatrice stroked the cat's head absently. Her mouth felt dry. She wet her lips with her tongue and blew her bangs out of her eyes. Still looking at her mother's face, Beatrice asked, "Why did she leave?"

"We'd better wait for Primrose," Laurel said uneasily. "I promised not to talk about your mother until Prim got home. Actually, we aren't supposed to discuss her at all."

Beatrice raised questioning eyes to her great-aunt's face. Laurel looked uncomfortable, and apologetic. "Once a witch is banished," Laurel said gently, "it's as if she never existed. We aren't allowed to mention her again."

Beatrice felt a wave of sadness wash over her, followed instantly by anger. *What right did anyone have to say her mother had never existed?* Was this some rule made up by the Witches' Executive Committee? By Aura Featherstone?

Beatrice's eyes darted back to the photograph. "That's Skye Drummond and Aura Featherstone with her. They look like they were best friends."

"They were," Laurel said. She bent down and kissed the top of Beatrice's head. "I have to get back to the shop. Primrose will be home later this afternoon. Will you be all right until then?"

Beatrice placed the photograph carefully on the table. Still looking at it, she said, "I'll be fine."

Laurel seemed troubled. Then suddenly her face lit up. "I just had a fantastic idea! Why don't the four of you come by the shop tomorrow and I'll design hats for you? I don't mean to brag," she added smugly, "but witches all over the Sphere are dying for a Laurel Merriwether original."

Teddy leaped up from her bed. "You mean it? You'll create hats just for us?"

"It will be my pleasure," Laurel assured her. "How does that sound to you, Beatrice?"

"I'd love one of your hats," Beatrice said.

Laurel appeared relieved. "Then it's a date. I've got to run, so make yourselves at home. Take a shower, rest, whatever. You'll find some games in the living room that might interest you."

After Laurel was gone, Beatrice went to the bathroom to bathe and change into lightweight clothes while Teddy unpacked. Beatrice was disappointed to see that there was no river nymph at Merriwether House; water ran out of faucets just like in the mortal world.

96

As she left the bathroom, Beatrice heard Teddy, Ollie, and Cyrus talking and laughing downstairs. She dashed to her bedroom to drop off her things before joining them—and stopped short in the doorway. There on his knees beside her bed was Bing. And he was going through her backpack!

Beatrice was staring in dismay at her clothes strewn all over the floor when Bing looked up and saw her. He leaped to his feet.

"What are you doing?" Beatrice demanded.

"Seeing if you have anything I'd want," Bing answered sullenly. "You don't," he added with a sneer. "There's nothing here but a bunch of junk."

"Pick up my clothes," Beatrice said, trying to control her temper. "Then fold them neatly."

"You think I'm your maid?" Bing shot back. "I got better things to do."

"I'm going to tell you one more time—"

"Tell me *twenty* times if you want," Bing shouted, scampering toward the window. "I just won't be around to hear you."

"Bing, come back here!"

But the boy had already disappeared through the window.

Beatrice ran across the room. She looked out the window and saw Bing shinnying down a rose trellis—and with such skill and confidence, she figured this must be a regular escape route. Beatrice watched as his feet hit the ground, and then he took off at a gallop.

Fuming, Beatrice blew her bangs out of her eyes and turned around to pick up her clothes. That's when she noticed the message. Hazy gray script floated across the dresser mirror, looking like it had been written in smoke. The words leaped out at her.

I'm so glad that you're finally here. I've been waiting for you.

The message was signed *Dally Rumpe*.

10

A Little Bit of Magic

Beatrice ran downstairs to tell the others about the message from Dally Rumpe—if, in fact, it *was* Dally Rumpe who had left it. Beatrice strongly suspected that Bing had left the sinister greeting to scare her.

Teddy, Ollie, and Cyrus were sitting around the table in the dining room playing a board game.

Ollie looked up when Beatrice came in and grinned. "Come see this, Beatrice. You won't believe it."

Beatrice went over to join them and Ollie noticed her subdued expression. "What is it?" he asked, his brow wrinkling in concern.

"I just found Bing going through my backpack," Beatrice said.

Ollie looked relieved. "Oh, is that all? I mean, he shouldn't have done that but—"

"We'll ask your aunts if there's a way to lock the door to our room," Teddy said. Then she looked down at the board and giggled. Ollie and Cyrus had turned their attention back to the game, as well, and were laughing uproariously.

"But that's not all," Beatrice said, having to raise her voice to be heard over the laughter. She frowned, annoyed by their silliness—when she had something *alarming* to tell them. "There was a message on the mirror!" she shouted. "It was signed *Dally Rumpe*."

Three heads jerked up to look at her. *Now* she had their attention.

Cyrus's eyes opened wide. "Did you say Dally Rumpe?"

"What did the message say?" Teddy asked.

Her irritation fading now that they were listening with the appropriate gravity, Beatrice said calmly, "Something like 'I'm glad you're finally here. I've been waiting for you.'"

"We're probably safe as long as we're in the village, don't you think?" Teddy said thoughtfully.

"Dally Rumpe has strong powers," Ollie said. "He might be able to get to us even here."

"I'm not even positive the message was left by Dally Rumpe," Beatrice admitted.

Cyrus looked puzzled. "But you said—"

"It was signed with his name," Beatrice said hastily, "but Bing had just been there when I saw the message."

"So you think it was Bing's idea of a joke?" Ollie asked.

Beatrice shook her head. "I don't know. It probably was Bing. But it's made me jittery."

"Some joke," Teddy fumed. "We'll have to tell your Aunt Primrose, Beatrice. That kid is out of control."

"Well, you can't tell her now," Cyrus said reasonably,

"so come join us, Beatrice." He pulled out a chair for her. "We'll start a new game."

"I don't want to start a new game," Teddy protested. "I'm winning."

"You've bought two measly properties," Cyrus grumbled.

"Not measly," Teddy replied. "Abracadabra Avenue and Wizard's Way are expensive real estate."

"Yeah," Cyrus said, "and you're nearly bankrupt."

"Not a problem," Teddy answered smugly. "When you land on one of my properties and have to pay up, I'll be rolling in dough."

"What *is* this game?" Beatrice asked, looking down at the board. Then she saw one of the pewter tokens move all by itself from Apparition Alley to Lucky Lane. Beatrice blinked.

"It's Witchopoly," Ollie said. "Come on and play, Beatrice. It's fun."

Beatrice was still staring at the board. She had just realized that *all* the tokens were moving. The tiny unicorn was pawing the board, the witch's hat was spinning like a tiny tornado, and the broomstick was doing a little sweeping dance.

"These tokens are *alive*," Beatrice said.

"Wait till you see what happens when you go to jail," Cyrus told her, his blue eyes twinkling merrily. "Little bitty goblin claws grab your token and drop it in the clinker."

Beatrice laughed and pulled her chair up to the table. "Okay, Teddy, keep your piddling real estate. Somebody give me some money—I'm going after Bewitchment Boulevard."

Two hours later, when Primrose and Molly arrived home, Beatrice was winning, with Ollie a close second. They had covered the board with haunted houses—which groaned and shrieked whenever someone's token landed on the property—and were going for hotels. Cyrus was having a great time, but Teddy was pouting. Forget about having fun, she wanted to *win*!

"Oh, good," Primrose said, "you found the games." She came and peered over Beatrice's shoulder at the board. "I'm glad no one used the banshee token. Not only is she a screecher, but she's been known to cheat. Molly, why don't you show them how to play Hangman the Witches' Sphere way?"

"Maybe later, Miss Primrose," Molly said. "I need to start dinner."

"We can get by with sandwiches tonight," Primrose said. "What about serpent's egg salad?"

Molly grinned. "You know Miss Laurel would have a fit if I served her a sandwich for dinner. I was thinking of a dandelion salad with black beetle dressing and horned toad in marigold sauce."

Cyrus gulped. His face had a definite green cast to it. "Don't go to any extra trouble for me," he said weakly.

"It's no trouble at all," Molly said cheerfully.

"Has anyone seen Bing?" Primrose asked.

"I hope he's in his room," Molly said. "He was supposed to come straight home from the witch academy and start studying for his Witch Etiquette test. That's his worst subject."

This information didn't surprise Beatrice. She wouldn't expect *any* kind of etiquette to be his strong point.

"Speaking of Bing," Beatrice said, "I found him going through the things in my backpack this afternoon."

"Bell, book, and candle," Primrose muttered. Then she sighed. "I'm sorry, Beatrice. I'll speak to him about it."

Then Beatrice told Primrose and Molly about the message on the mirror.

Primrose looked startled. "And you think Bing did it?"

"I don't know, Aunt Primrose." Beatrice frowned. She believed that Bing could use a little discipline—well, maybe a *lot* of discipline—but she didn't want him to get in trouble for something he hadn't done.

"I don't think he did it."

They all turned to look at Molly.

"Bing wouldn't even know how to write a message in smoke," Molly said. "Besides, he can be infuriating, but he isn't really bad. I don't think he'd try to frighten you with a message from Dally Rumpe."

Beatrice wasn't so sure about that.

"Molly, sit down," Primrose said briskly. "I think we need to tell them about Bing."

When they were all seated around the table, Primrose said, "Bing is an orphan. He's the son of an evil witch named Morag and an oath breaker warlock named Cosmo —and as we know, *all* warlocks are evil. They lived in a hovel at the edge of the swamp, and there was no end to the wicked things they did. It was rumored that they made their living by luring innocent travelers into the swamps and robbing then, then leaving them to wander aimlessly until they fell into quicksand or died of starvation. Some even thought it was their lanterns that moved through the swamps at night."

"Only we still see the lights," Molly pointed out.

"Yes, we do," Primrose agreed brightly. "But back to Bing. His parents had heard that Bromwich's daughter Innes had a fortune in gold hidden away in Werewolf Close. I think it's just part of the legend that's grown up around Innes, but over the years we've all heard tales of witches—always nameless, of course—who supposedly made it into the Close and managed to steal some of the gold. According to the stories, the thief usually had just enough time to bury the treasure in the swamp before a tragic accident took his or her life. To this day, some people believe there are chests of gold coins to be found in those swamps. Anyway, being the greedy witch and warlock that they were, Morag and Cosmo searched the swamps for years trying to find the gold. Without success. They decided the treasure must still be inside Werewolf Close, so they cast a spell that they thought would transport them safely into the Close. But they were devoured by the werewolves. Some swamp dwellers heard the ferocious growling and the screams soon after Morag and Cosmo entered the fog."

Fear settled heavily on Beatrice's chest, making it hard for her to take a deep breath. She looked around the table at Teddy, Ollie, and Cyrus, and saw by their fixed expressions that they, too, were afraid.

"Bing had no other family," Primrose continued, "and no one in the village wanted him because of his parents. They assume that he must be evil, too. That's why he does bad things," Primrose said with a hint of sadness, "to live up to his reputation. But I haven't seen evidence that he has any power. Sometimes it happens that way and skips a generation."

Primrose paused and looked at their faces. "Oh, my," she said. "I shouldn't have mentioned the werewolves." Then she added briskly, "But maybe it's just as well. I wanted to talk to you about your trip to Werewolf Close, anyway. Now is probably as good a time as any."

"What is there to talk about?" Beatrice asked her great-aunt.

"Whether you should go or not," Primrose said bluntly, "and I say you shouldn't. You've already shown how brave you are by breaking the spell on Winter Wood. The *next* Bailiwick witch can work on Werewolf Close."

"Aunt Primrose," Beatrice said gently, "it took two hundred years for the first part of the spell to be broken. At this rate, it would be—let's see—eight hundred years before the other four parts are reversed."

"The time will fly by! And you've done as much as anyone can expect you to do," Primrose said, a hint of stubbornness creeping into her voice. "Forget about Werewolf Close! You can stay here in Friar's Lantern— *all* of you can stay—and have a wonderful life."

An alarm went off inside Beatrice's head. Her mother had *said* the aunts would try to convince Beatrice to stay with them.

"But then we'd lose our one chance to become Classical witches," Teddy responded. Her expression plainly said that she didn't consider that an option.

"So what?" Primrose shot back. "Do you know how few Classical witches there are in the Sphere? Old Yorick Figlock is one of a half dozen in Friar's Lantern, and he's got bubbles in the think tank. Then there's Skye Drummond, but she stopped using her powers years ago and barely makes ends meet with that shop of hers. I can't see that being a Classical witch has made either of them wildly successful."

"I thought maybe you were Classical," Teddy mumbled, looking embarrassed. "The way you flew down off the roof today . . ."

"Me? *Classical?*" Primrose's laugh came out sounding like a prolonged snort. "I'm Everyday and proud of it," she said stoutly. "That little flying trick is nothing. Any witch in the Sphere can perform small magic, like floating down from the roof or turning a basket of strawberries into jam, but most don't have any real talent. We just have a *little bit* of magic."

Teddy looked devastated. "Then what's the point of living in the Witches' Sphere if you're all Everyday witches?" she demanded.

Primrose seemed surprised. "Why, because it's fun! And when you're surrounded by magic," she added, "you pick up a little more power for yourself. It kind of seeps in."

Teddy was frowning. "Well, I don't think making jam is very good magic," she grumbled.

About that time, Bing came through the front door. Seeing everyone gathered around the table, he tried to tiptoe up the stairs without being noticed. But Primrose caught him on the third step.

"Bing, come in here please!" Primrose bellowed.

Bing slunk into the dining room, scowling.

Primrose regarded him sternly. "You owe Beatrice an apology. And make it *sincere.*"

Bing shot Beatrice a furious look. "I might have known you'd tattle!"

"Bing." Primrose's expression left no room for argument.

Bing glanced from Primrose to Beatrice. Everyone waited in silence for him to speak.

"*All right*," Bing snarled. "I'm sorry I went through your things. I won't do it again."

"And?" Primrose prompted.

Bing looked surprised. "And what?" he demanded. "I *said* I wouldn't do it again."

"The message," Primrose said.

"What message?" Bing seemed genuinely confused.

Beatrice felt her pulse quicken. "You didn't leave a message in my room?" she asked.

"No way!" Bing was scowling again. "Why does everybody blame me for everything that happens around here?"

"Perhaps," Primrose said with a meaningful lift of her eyebrows, "because you try so hard to make everyone think you're bad."

"Oh. Well, I *am* bad," he said hastily. "But I didn't leave any message. You can believe me or not. I don't care!" Then he stomped out of the room and ran up the stairs.

There was silence as they stared after him. Finally Beatrice said, "I believe him."

"So do I," Primrose said, and she sounded worried.

Beatrice and her friends were so tired after their full day, they nearly fell asleep over dinner. Primrose suggested they get ready for bed. "I'll be up in a few minutes to say good night," she said.

Beatrice and Teddy put on their nightgowns and crawled into their soft feather beds. Cayenne settled in the crook of Beatrice's arm with her head on Beatrice's shoulder. Beatrice was determined to question Primrose about her mother's banishment and fully intended to stay awake until her great-aunt came in. But only moments after going to bed, Beatrice drifted off to sleep.

Two hours later, Beatrice woke up with a start. Cayenne was standing at the end of the bed, staring out the window and growling softly.

There was a rustling from Teddy's bed, then Teddy's sleepy voice was saying, "What's wrong with Cayenne?"

Before Beatrice could answer, there came a soft scraping sound from outside, then a muffled *clunk* as something struck the side of the house.

Beatrice and Teddy were wide awake now. They bolted out of bed and ran to the window. Beatrice pointed to a spot several yards away where a dark figure was slowly descending the trellis. She thought it had to be Bing—and sure enough, when the climber turned his head slightly, there was Bing's face illuminated in the moonlight.

A soft knock on the door caused Beatrice and Teddy to jump. Then the door opened and they saw that it was only Ollie and Cyrus.

"We heard noises," Ollie said softly as he and Cyrus joined the girls at the window.

"It's Bing," Beatrice whispered.

They all peered out the window, and as they watched the boy drop to the ground, a taller figure stepped out from the shrubbery that ran along the edge of the garden. Beatrice could tell it was a man, but she couldn't see his face. Then they heard Bing saying, "I was afraid you wouldn't wait. Let's get out of here, Xan, before they catch me."

Xan Renshaw!

"What's Bing doing with a smuggler?" Teddy whispered.

"Maybe Bing isn't as innocent as Primrose believes he is," Ollie replied.

"She does seem to think the best of everyone," Beatrice mused.

"Let's follow them," Cyrus suggested.

"Are you nuts?" Ollie responded. "First, it could be dangerous, and second, Bing and Xan don't have anything to do with our reason for being here."

"How do we know that?" Teddy asked quickly. "They could be working for Dally Rumpe. Or one of them might even *be* Dally Rumpe. That would explain Beatrice seeing the message right after Bing was here."

"We're wasting time talking," Cyrus said impatiently. "If we don't hurry, we'll lose them."

"I think we should go after them," Beatrice said, and Ollie reluctantly agreed.

Cayenne was already out the window. She grabbed the trellis with her claws and started down. Beatrice and her friends weren't as agile as Bing and the cat, and it took a while for them all to climb down to the ground.

"They're gone," Cyrus said, looking around the shadowy garden in disappointment. "We'll never find them now."

Then Beatrice noticed Cayenne heading into the woods behind the house. "I think she knows which way they went," Beatrice said.

It was peculiar following a cat across the dark landscape. Cayenne could slip through narrow openings between trees and walk under low-growing bushes. Beatrice and her friends found themselves running into branches, tripping over roots, and stepping into holes in their clumsy attempts to keep up with the cat. They were feeling bruised, battered, and sweaty by the time the cat led them out to Will-o'-the-wisp Road just below the wharf.

Cayenne came to a stop and stared across the road.

"There they are," Beatrice whispered, watching as two figures slipped silently into the swamp. She stooped down and stroked Cayenne. "You're such a smart cat," she said.

"Come on," Teddy said.

"Wait, Teddy." Cyrus reached out and grabbed her arm.

"Wait for what?" Teddy asked impatiently.

"I don't think we should go into the swamp at night."

Teddy spun around to face him. "Good grief, Cyrus! It was your idea to follow them in the first place. You can't chicken out now."

"I'm not chickening out!" Cyrus exclaimed. "But I don't want to get lost in there, either. Remember what Primrose said about people falling into quicksand?"

"Cyrus is right," Ollie said quietly. "It's too dangerous."

"But if we stop now, we won't have accomplished

anything," Teddy protested. "I'll have gotten all these scratches and bug bites for nothing."

Just then, Cayenne meowed sharply. She was gazing at the swamp across the river. Beatrice and her friends looked in the same direction and saw what Cayenne had been trying to tell them. A half-dozen pale bluish lights were moving slowly through the swamp.

Beatrice's heart sped up. "Well, we know that isn't Xan," she said softly. "He and Bing are on this side of the river."

They watched as the lights moved deeper into the dense growth, growing smaller and dimmer—until finally, they disappeared.

11

The Mad Witch

As Beatrice and her friends were walking to The Cat and the Fiddle for breakfast the next morning, Beatrice announced, "I want to go to Werewolf Close."

Teddy gave her a look. "Isn't that why we're here?"

"No, I mean I want to go *now*," Beatrice said. "Just to find out where it is. I think those lights last night might have been heading there."

"Sounds good to me," Teddy said promptly. Then she frowned. "But would we get into trouble with the Witches' Executive Committee if we don't wait for their instructions? I don't want to blow my chance to become Classical."

"We wouldn't be going inside," Beatrice said reasonably. "How can the committee object to us just walking past it?"

"Your Aunt Laurel warned us not to wander around on our own," Ollie pointed out.

Beatrice grinned. "You mean like we did last night. This time we'll go in the daylight."

"Let's do it," Cyrus said. "How do we get a boat?"

"We can ask someone at the wharf," Beatrice replied. "But don't mention this to Aunt Primrose and Aunt Laurel. No need to worry them."

Most of the court cats were gathered at the back of the restaurant. Beatrice understood why when she saw Molly placing bowls outside the door. The cats swarmed around Molly, rubbing against her legs and sending forth a chorus of excited meows. Cayenne started toward them, but Beatrice grabbed her.

"You'll eat inside with us," Beatrice informed the cat.

They had just finished ordering breakfast when Fillian Hawthorn came in. He saw them and waved, then headed for their table.

"All of a sudden, I don't feel so hungry," Ollie muttered.

Beatrice shot him a look. "What is it with you and Fillian?"

"He's a phony," Ollie answered curtly.

It wasn't like Ollie to criticize—especially someone he barely knew—but Beatrice didn't have time to question him. Fillian had arrived at the table and was bringing over a chair to sit beside Beatrice.

Teddy glanced thoughtfully at Ollie, then at Beatrice. "I think I get it," she murmured.

"So how was your first night in Friar's Lantern?" Fillian asked Beatrice.

"Eventful," Teddy responded before Beatrice could speak.

Fillian gave Teddy a questioning look.

"What she means," Beatrice said hastily, "is that we had an interesting visit with my great-aunts."

"Right," Teddy said. "Oh, good. Here comes Glee—or is it Puddifoot?—with our food."

"You call scrambled serpent's eggs *food?*" Cyrus demanded.

"Honestly, Cyrus, you are so *mortal*," Teddy said in exasperation.

"Are you working today?" Beatrice asked Fillian.

He nodded. "This morning I'm reading to a couple of witches and taking Penelope Gall's pet salamander to the vet for its shots. And after lunch I have to deliver some groceries to Yorick Figlock."

Beatrice looked up, fork poised in the air. "Didn't you say that Yorick lives across the river? Is that anywhere near Werewolf Close?"

"In its shadow, actually," Fillian replied. Glee had brought him a plate heaped with serpent's eggs and sour milk biscuits. He smiled his thanks and reached for the rose petal jelly. Then he sprinkled honeyed ants across his eggs.

"Would it be possible for us to go with you to visit Yorick?" Beatrice asked him.

Fillian looked surprised. After a brief hesitation, he said, "I suppose it would be all right. Can you meet me at the wharf at two o'clock?"

Cyrus grinned. Teddy gave her friend an admiring look. Ollie appeared grumpier than ever.

Fillian hurried through his breakfast and left. The others were finishing up when Primrose came over to the table and asked how they planned to spend their day.

"We're going to Laurel's shop," Teddy said. "She's offered to design hats for us."

Primrose looked amused. "Just let me warn you, Laurel's hats are usually rather large and—*dramatic*. So what else do you have planned?"

"We'll probably check out the other shops in the court," Beatrice said, not adding that she wanted to meet Skye Drummond and see if the witch would say anything about her mother.

"Just don't go to The Muddy Duck," Primrose said.

Beatrice had no desire to see that ill-mannered Nobby Chinwhisker again, but Primrose's warning had made her curious. "Why shouldn't we go there?" she asked.

"You saw for yourself that Nobby's sly and uncouth," Primrose said, "and we don't know much about him. He hasn't been here very long. But I've seen some rough witches from the swamp going into the pub, and I don't want you associating with that crowd."

Teddy couldn't wait to see Laurel's shop, so they went to Head in the Clouds first. As soon as Beatrice walked through the front door, she noticed her Great-aunt Laurel's elegant touch everywhere. From the pale blue-gray walls—obviously, Laurel's signature color—to the striking displays. Traditional pointed witches' hats in silks and velvets sat in cloudlike nests of silver tulle. Beatrice was drawn to a witch's hat made of midnight blue velvet. The brim was turned up jauntily on one side and held with a silver cat pin. She wandered past feathered turbans that reminded her of tropical birds, romantic bonnets covered with roses and satin ribbon, and beanies trimmed with glittering beads. There were black silk top hats, berets accented with tulips and poppies, and hats made to look like dragons and other fanciful beasts.

Laurel came through a door at the back of the shop and beamed at them. "Welcome to Head in the Clouds," she said grandly, "where all your wishes can come true."

"Your hats are gorgeous," Teddy said, peering around the shop with an expression of pure bliss. "That tangerine satin witch's hat—and the black velvet beret with the poppies—*ohhhh*, and I *love* the red one with black ribbon and silver beads."

Beatrice grinned. She could see that Teddy would be content to stay here all day, and Laurel would be delighted to have her. Ollie and Cyrus, on the other hand, appeared vaguely uncomfortable.

"Now, each of you must tell me which hats appeal to you so I'll have some ideas when I start my designs," Laurel said.

"I want something like the red one," Teddy said. "But maybe with netting. And the poppies are very smart. Or do you think," Teddy added, beginning to look distressed, "that a plain witch's hat might be better? In satin—no, velvet. Actually, a witch's hat might be *too* plain."

Ollie rolled his eyes, and Cyrus gazed longingly at the door. Beatrice decided they needed to speed this up.

"I like the blue velvet witch's hat," Beatrice said. "The one with the silver cat pin. Could I try it on, Aunt Laurel?"

"Of course you may," Laurel said. She lifted the hat tenderly and placed it on Beatrice's head, fussing with her niece's hair and adjusting the crown with a critical eye. "There," Laurel said, and stood back to study the effect. "It's smashing!" she proclaimed. "The simplicity suits you."

Beatrice looked at herself in the closest mirror. The

color was nice with her red hair, and she loved the way the brim dipped over her left eye.

"This is the one I want," Beatrice said.

"Then you shall have it," Laurel said promptly.

"I love it, Aunt Laurel. Thank you."

Ollie took Beatrice's lead. "I think I'd like one of those," he said, pointing to a simple black top hat.

"Yeah," Cyrus said quickly. "Me, too."

They found one that fit Ollie right away, but all the top hats were too large for Cyrus and slid down over his eyes.

"I can stuff paper in it or something," Cyrus said with a touch of desperation, after he had tried on the fifth hat.

"We can't have that." Laurel looked horrified. "I'll create one that will fit you perfectly. Let me take the measurements." A tape measure floated up from the counter and landed in her hand.

"Well, I want something made especially for me," Teddy said. "This may be my only chance to have a designer hat."

Realizing that it could take hours for Teddy to make up her mind, Beatrice said, "Ollie and Cyrus and I wanted to look in the other shops, Teddy. Is it okay if we go on and meet you at the restaurant for lunch?"

Teddy frowned. She never wanted to be left out of anything, but she wasn't about to make a quick decision on something as important as a hat. "Sure," Teddy said grudgingly. "You guys go on."

"Don't be late for lunch," Beatrice said. "*Remember*, we have a busy afternoon planned."

"Okay," Teddy answered, already turning away to examine a turban embroidered with silver moons and stars.

When Beatrice left the shop, swinging the blue-gray box that contained her hat, she nearly bumped into Xan Renshaw who was headed for The Muddy Duck next door.

"Excuse me," Beatrice said hastily.

Xan scowled and grunted. He brushed past her and was about to go inside the pub when Beatrice said to his retreating back, "I don't think we've met. I'm Beatrice Bailiwick."

Xan turned around. "I know who you are," he said crisply. "But isn't it time for you to stop playing the great witch and leave us alone?"

Beatrice stepped back, his words affecting her like a slap in the face. "There's no need to be—" But she never finished the sentence because Xan had jerked open the door to the pub and disappeared inside.

"He's a witch with an attitude," Ollie said as they crossed the court. "Don't let him bother you."

"I'm not bothered," Beatrice responded. But she couldn't help wondering why Xan Renshaw seemed so hostile toward her when he didn't even know her.

They opened the door to Maiden's Blush and were met with the scent of lavender. Skye Drummond was helping a customer select eyeshadow while a young witch in the back was cutting another customer's hair.

Cyrus took one look and stopped in the doorway. "I think I'll wait out here," he said.

"Sounds like a good idea," Ollie agreed.

"I won't be long," Beatrice told them, and strolled into the shop.

She went over to a shelf and pretended to study a display of herbal shampoos and conditioners, watching Skye out of the corner of her eye. Soon she heard Skye say, "Merry part, Eugenia. Come back soon." Then Skye walked over to Beatrice.

"May I help you?" the blond witch asked, her voice courteous but noticeably cool.

"I'm Beatrice Bailiwick."

"I know," Skye said with no change of expression. "Are you looking for something in particular?"

"Actually, I hoped you'd have time to talk with me," Beatrice said. "You knew my mother—Nina Merriwether."

Skye looked at her steadily. "Did she tell you that?"

Beatrice shook her head. "No, my Great-aunt Laurel did. She said that you and my mother were good friends."

Something flickered in Skye's eyes. "I thought we were *best* friends once," she said, her voice sounding distant. "But I was wrong."

Then, before Beatrice could respond, Skye turned abruptly and went to greet another customer.

Teddy showed up late for lunch, her face glowing as she hurried over to the table where Beatrice, Ollie, Cyrus, and Cayenne had already started eating.

"You decided on the perfect hat," Beatrice guessed.

"It's going to be breathtaking!" Teddy exclaimed. "I've never seen another hat like it in my life. But I can't tell you about it. You'll have to wait and see it."

"You're late," Cyrus informed her. "Stop talking about hats and order something. We have to meet Fillian in a few minutes."

At the mention of Fillian, Ollie looked down at his plate. *But at least he isn't glaring*, Beatrice thought. It had occurred to her that Ollie might be jealous because Fillian was being nice to her. But that was ridiculous! Fillian was way too old for her, and besides that, Ollie was too levelheaded for something as silly as jealousy.

Fillian was waiting for them at the pier with a small boat.

"Thanks for letting us come with you," Beatrice said, following Teddy into the boat. "We want to see some of the countryside while we're here."

"One *part* of the countryside, anyway," Fillian replied pleasantly. "Isn't that right?"

"For obvious reasons, we have a particular interest in Werewolf Close," Ollie said as he sat down beside Cyrus. Ollie's expression was bland, but Beatrice heard the edge in his voice.

A shadow crossed Fillian's face. "You can see the fog from Yorick's cabin," he said, "but I won't take you any closer than that."

Fillian raised his arm in an arc and the boat began to move away from the pier. As they sped across the river toward the opposite shore, Fillian turned to Beatrice, and said with concern, "I'm surprised that Miss Primrose and Miss Laurel haven't insisted that you give up on the idea of going to Werewolf Close. It's no place to play at magic."

Beatrice didn't care for his implication that they were just kids who didn't know what they were doing—even if he was right. She noticed Ollie watching her, eyebrows raised as if to say, *What did I tell you?*

But then Fillian was smiling again. "I shouldn't have expressed an opinion," he said quickly. "I know it's none of my business. But after meeting you four, I'd really hate to see anything happen to you."

"That's so nice of you to say," Teddy said, gushing a little. "Isn't it, Beatrice?"

"Nice," Beatrice murmured, but his words still rankled.

The boat pulled up to the shore and glided smoothly onto a crescent of sand. Fillian leaped out and extended a hand to Beatrice, then Teddy. Only a few feet away loomed the moss-draped trees and thick undergrowth of the swamp.

"There's a trail to Yorick's cabin," Fillian said. "Stay close behind me and don't step off the path. The ground might look solid, but you could sink in over your head before I have time to pull you out."

Fillian lifted a sack from the boat and started down a narrow trail of packed earth that led into the swamp. Beatrice and her friends followed obediently on his heels. Even Cayenne showed no inclination to leave the safe haven of Beatrice's arms.

Soon they had left the bright sunlight behind, burrowing deeper and deeper into the darkness of the swamp. Beatrice noticed that the ground began to feel spongy beneath her feet. The air was wet and heavy, smelling of dampness and rotting vegetation. Occasionally, through breaks in the undergrowth, she saw water standing near the path. *There must be snakes in that water*, Beatrice thought, *and overhead in the trees*. She glanced up warily, and then it occurred to her that there might be something worse than a snake lurking nearby. She shuddered, wondering why she had ever gotten them into this.

Beatrice lost track of time. She just knew they had been walking for a long time when Fillian suddenly stopped.

"That's where Yorick lives," Fillian said.

Beatrice saw the rough unpainted walls of a small cabin squatting in a tangle of brush and vines.

"And there," Fillian added, pointing beyond the cabin, "is Werewolf Close."

Hovering above the swamp like a gigantic mass of storm clouds was the fog. But even if she hadn't known its significance, Beatrice was sure that she would have felt the evil emanating from the dense gray mist. At a distance of a hundred yards or more, she found the enchanted fog menacing.

"Well, we wanted to see it," Cyrus said in a small voice.

"This is worse than the hedge of thorns at Winter Wood," Teddy added.

Beatrice agreed. Because they had been able to see what they were up against with the hedge. As formidable as it had been, the hedge of thorns had a beginning and an end. This fog whirled and shifted and changed shapes all the time, as if it were a living thing. It seemed to be— everywhere!

"I won't take you any closer," Fillian interrupted their somber thoughts. "Shall we go see Yorick now? And don't put too much stock in anything he says. Sometimes he's a bit addled."

Beatrice nodded, grateful to be leaving the ring of fog. *How can we possibly find our way through it?* she wondered, walking in a daze toward the cabin.

Fillian went to the open front door and called out to Yorick before stepping inside. Beatrice and the others followed him, ducking to avoid vines that covered the roof and spilled over the doorway.

The cabin had a dirt floor and was sparsely furnished, but it appeared surprisingly neat and orderly. Beatrice noted that the hearth had been swept clean of ashes and the cot in the corner had been made up with fresh sheets. Then her eyes fell on the man in faded robes who sat hunched over a table in the center of the room. Long gray hair fell in tangles past his bony shoulders and a beard that could have used a trim covered most of his face. While Beatrice studied him, the man stared back at her with pale gray eyes that seemed too bright.

"Yorick, let me introduce my friends," Fillian said as he lowered the sack to the table.

"No need," Yorick answered hoarsely. "I know who this is," he said, jerking his head toward Beatrice.

Suddenly there was a loud squawk from a shadowy corner. Beatrice and her friends jumped, and Cayenne growled softly in her throat.

Yorick slapped the top of the table with his hands, startling his visitors further, and then he laughed. It was the delirious braying of a madman!

Beatrice noticed that Yorick was missing most of his teeth. Then her eyes fell on the corded pink skin showing above his beard. The left side of his face was horribly scarred, as were his hands. His left arm was held at an odd angle, as if it had been broken and hadn't been set properly.

"Old Foxy scared you, didn't he?" Yorick grinned at Beatrice, then glanced at the corner of the room.

Beatrice followed his gaze and saw a large gray bird on a perch, nearly hidden in the shadows. As if to reward her for finding him, the bird squawked again.

"That'll be enough, Old Foxy," Yorick said, no longer grinning and sounding querulous. "How's an old witch supposed to know what he's thinking with you carrying on like that?"

Fillian was taking food out of the sack and stacking it in a cupboard. Beatrice and her friends stood by the door looking uncertain.

How can I bring up the subject of Werewolf Close? Beatrice thought. She couldn't just ask him if he'd ever been there, could she? Then she realized that he was staring at her again. The look he gave her was shrewd, as if he were weighing something in his mind. At that moment, Beatrice had the uncanny feeling that Yorick Figlock was completely lucid. And that he not only knew who she was, but also why she had come to Friar's Lantern.

"Do you get lonely out here without any neighbors?" Beatrice asked him, as a means of starting a conversation.

He grinned slyly. "That's not what you want to ask, is it?" he said. "I've got answers. You just have to ask the right questions."

Fillian glanced over at Yorick and then at Beatrice. He shrugged discreetly, as if to say, *I told you he's mad. Makes no sense at all.*

Suddenly Yorick held out his scarred left hand and Old

124

Foxy flew over and landed on his finger. The witch smiled fondly at the bird.

"Who needs neighbors when I've got him?" Yorick demanded. "But he's more than company. He's my eyes and my ears. The compass that keeps me on course." Yorick looked straight at Beatrice. That crafty smile reappeared. "*My compass, my guide*," he said, the words coming out like a hiss of steam.

Beatrice was almost certain that he was trying to tell her something, but she had no idea what.

"Your compass," she said, her eyes locked with his.

He nodded. "My guide," he repeated softly.

"Well, Yorick," Fillian said suddenly, "is there anything else you need? I'll be coming back day after tomorrow."

Yorick frowned, as if Fillian had annoyed him. He dropped his eyes from Beatrice's and stared into space.

Beatrice nearly cried out, *What is it you're trying to tell me?* But Fillian was saying good-bye to Yorick and the others were filing out of the cabin. Beatrice followed them reluctantly.

Then Yorick called out suddenly, "Beatrice Bailiwick!"

Beatrice spun around. The old witch's pale eyes bored into her face.

"Listen to me," he said urgently. "There are two things you need."

When he didn't continue, Beatrice said quickly, "What two things?"

"You need a guide," Yorick said. "And you need courage."

Beatrice waited for Yorick to continue, but he said no

more. Then Fillian called Beatrice's name from outside. "Are you ready? We should be heading back."

Beatrice started for the door, feeling disappointed and confused. She had been sure that Yorick Figlock was going to tell her something important—but if he had, she didn't understand it.

Beatrice paused in the doorway and looked back. "Merry part," she said.

But Yorick was engrossed in a conversation with Old Foxy and didn't respond.

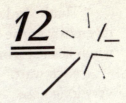

12

Secrets Revealed

When Beatrice and her friends arrived home, they met Molly coming out the front door. Her eyes lingered on the leaves and Spanish moss in their hair, then dropped to their shoes, which were wet and stained from the swamp. But all Molly said was, "I'm on my way to pick up Bing for a dental appointment. Do you want to come with me and see the witch academy?"

"You bet!" Teddy exclaimed.

Ollie and Cyrus nodded. "I've always wanted to see a witch academy," Ollie said.

So had Beatrice, although what she wanted most at the moment was a shower and clean clothes. But since the others were anxious to go, Beatrice said, "That sounds good."

The witch academy—officially called WA 113—was on Will-o'-the-wisp Road, just around the corner from Cattail Court. It was an old two-story building made of gray stone, wedged in between Friar's Lantern Public Library and Tail Winds Broom Shop. In front of the witch academy was a large stone statue of a skinny witch holding an open book.

"That's Lydwina Pantaloonie," Molly said, gazin
reverently at the stern-faced statue. "She founded the firs
witch academy in Friar's Lantern."

"Nice wart," Cyrus murmured, peering at the statue
very long nose.

Molly led them up the front steps and into a narro
hallway that was shrouded in cobwebs and smelled of dus
and sulfur.

Molly took a deep satisfied breath. "Oh, this takes m
back," she said. "I was a student here through sixth grad
Then they classified me Everyday, so I had to leave. Thos
were the best years!" she added fervently.

Teddy ducked to avoid a large spider that had droppe
down from the ceiling, then looked around in disma
Her expression clearly said that this wasn't what she ha
expected.

Molly stopped at one of the classroom doors. "We
here we are. Bing's class is working on healing potions th
afternoon," she said gravely. "The healing arts are seriou
business."

About that time, they heard a loud commotion fro
inside the classroom. Peering through the glass in the doc
they saw chaos. One girl was hopping around like a kar
garoo and another was howling like a wolf. Two studen
were at least ten feet tall, while others were the size
chipmunks. A boy was floating across the ceiling with
stunned expression on his face, and several more we
jumping around scratching themselves and screamin
"Fleas! Ticks! Get 'em off me!"

Then Beatrice saw Makepeace Drummond—wl
looked perfectly normal except for the purple hair stan

ing straight up on his head—chasing Bing around the room, screeching, "You switched the potions! *Just wait till I catch you!*"

Bing was leaping over desks and laughing. He seemed to be having the time of his life.

Primrose was in a bad mood that night. First she chewed Bing out and sent him to his room without dinner. Then she turned a grim face to Beatrice and her friends.

"It's all over the village that you four went to Werewolf Close this afternoon," Primrose said.

"No, Aunt Primrose," Beatrice said truthfully. "We went to visit Yorick Figlock. We could see the fog from his cabin, but we didn't go near it."

"You were close enough," Primrose snapped. "Have you received your instructions from the Witches' Executive Committee?"

"No, ma'am."

"Then what are you doing wandering around in the swamp?" Primrose demanded.

Laurel had been pretending to look at a fashion magazine. Now she gave up the charade and threw the magazine aside. "Prim, you've got to expect them to be curious about the Close. And *you* were the one who told them all that bunk about Yorick making it inside."

Primrose glared at her sister. Then she said to Beatrice, "Well, I suppose that's true. But you still shouldn't be nosing around out there until you get directions from the committee."

Just then, Molly peeked around the doorway. "I've fixed a picnic dinner," she said, her bright eyes darting from Primrose to the others. "I thought we could all use a change of pace."

"Thank you, Molly," Primrose said stiffly.

"I love moonlit dinners!" Laurel exclaimed. "Molly, bring your flute and play for us."

"What about Bing?" Molly asked.

"All right," Primrose said, still sounding out of sorts. "He can come down to eat. I guess we can't have him starving to death."

"Dinner will be ready in ten minutes," Molly said, and started up the stairs after Bing.

"I'm getting soft in my old age," Primrose muttered.

Laurel grinned and put an arm around her sister's shoulder. "Only where your lost sheep are concerned. Come on, you old bat, let's kick off our shoes and get ready to dance by the light of the moon."

Beatrice had never been to a picnic like this. A table in the backyard had been covered with a lace cloth and set with candles and the Merriwether sisters' best china and silver, leading Beatrice to expect more of Molly's gourmet delights. But Molly brought out trays piled high with hexburgers, devil dogs, fury fries, and pitchers of iced moonbeam tea. For dessert, they had devil's food cake and fruit-fly custard. When they were all too full to eat another bite—except for Bing, who kept snitching more cake—Molly sat down in the grass and began to play her flute.

The melody was soft and ethereal, casting a gentle

spell over the listeners. Beatrice lay back and gazed into the night sky, feeling content and drowsy as the dreamlike music washed over her and then soared to meet the stars.

After a while, the music stopped abruptly. Then Molly began to play a piece with a strange and enticing rhythm that made Beatrice want to leap to her feet and dance. She noticed that Primrose and Laurel had done just that. The two sisters were cavorting across the lawn in the moonlight, swaying and bending and spinning in time to the music. Soon Beatrice and her friends had joined them. They danced and laughed until they were breathless, and then one by one, they collapsed. Stretching out in the soft grass, Beatrice felt light and happy and exquisitely alive.

Primrose had fallen near Molly. She raised herself up on her elbows and said to the girl, "You have so many talents, my dear. I'm afraid you'll want more than Friar's Lantern can offer."

"What more could I want?" Molly asked, and started loading a tray with dishes to carry inside.

"How about a little fun?" Beatrice suggested. "All you do is work."

Molly looked surprised. "Cooking and music aren't work," she said, and headed for the house with the tray.

"Off to bed with you," Primrose said to Beatrice and her friends as they walked into the living room.

Beatrice was tired, but the inviting feather bed upstairs would have to wait. "Tell me about my mother," she said.

Primrose and Laurel seemed to freeze where they stood.

"Come on, Bing," Molly said briskly, guiding him gently toward the stairs.

"I want to stay," he protested. "This is going to be good."

"Go to bed, Bing," Primrose said firmly.

"Aw, gee," Bing muttered, and started heavily up the stairs with Molly behind him.

Beatrice sat down on the sofa and looked up at Primrose, waiting.

Primrose sighed. "All right," she said, and sat down beside Beatrice.

The others came to join them.

"Beatrice, do you want us to leave?" Ollie asked.

Beatrice shook her head. "No, you can hear this."

Brows furrowed, Primrose said, "Your mother came to visit us when she was sixteen. She loved Friar's Lantern and decided to stay. She was very popular with the young witches here, and became especially close to Aura Featherstone and Skye Littlejohn—Drummond now that she's married." Primrose paused, thinking. "You need to know something about Aura and Skye in order to understand your mother. They had both been classified Classical the same year, which was quite a coup for this little village, and were very competitive. They wanted to be the greatest witches in the world."

Beatrice glanced at Teddy, who dropped her eyes, looking sheepish.

"They were taking courses in advanced magic at the witch academy when your mother came to Friar's Lantern," Primrose continued. "The three girls hit it off right away and Nina wanted to do everything that Aura and Skye did."

Beatrice wondered if Primrose was aware that she had

spoken Nina's name. Was this the first time anyone had said *Nina* aloud since she was banished?

"Nina had been classified Everyday," Primrose went on, "but Aura and Skye thought that was because she had grown up in the mortal world. So they came up with a plan to prove that Nina was worthy of a Classical classification."

"You need to tell them about Xan Renshaw's father and mother," Laurel interrupted.

"I was getting to that," Primrose said, frowning in her sister's direction. "Yes, well—Gil Renshaw, Xan's father, was a notorious smuggler. For years, he had been bringing in poisonous herbs and other nasty things for witches in the swamps to use in their dark magic. Everyone knew it, but nobody had been able to catch him. Gil's wife, Thera, was involved in the smuggling, too, but Gil was the mastermind. So Aura and Skye came up with a plan to catch Gil in the act. Using what they had learned at the witch academy, they wrote two spells—one to locate Gil when he was up to no good, and one for Nina to recite that was supposed to immobilize him until the authorities could get there and see the evidence of his smuggling."

"And don't forget to tell her that Nina was supposed to wait for Aura and Skye," Laurel said. Then she added to Beatrice, "Aura and Skye wanted to be there in case your mother had any problems."

"But Nina decided to show her friends that she could do it all on her own," Primrose said. "She went to the swamp, recited the location spell, and found Gil and Thera—along with everything from deadly felonwort and enchanter's nightshade to a gallon of dragon's blood. Good witches don't kill creatures for the sake of their magic," Primrose said fiercely, "so that was a terrible thing for them to have. Anyway, your mother recited the spell to immobilize Gil, but something went wrong. It was Thera who was immobilized with all the evidence, while Gil ran off into the swamp. Thera was arrested, tried, and found guilty. She died soon after being banished from the Sphere."

Despite the heat, Beatrice felt a sudden chill. Xan had grown up without ever knowing his mother all because of Nina Bailey's spell. Beatrice understood now why Xan despised her and accused her of playing *the great witch*. Because wasn't that what her mother had done?

Seeing the distress in Beatrice's face, Primrose said gently, "You know your mother didn't mean to harm Thera. In fact, Nina was convinced that there was a flaw in the spell Aura and Skye had written. Aura and Skye claimed the problem was in Nina's recitation. Skye, in particular, was very angry with Nina. Aura was more mature about it and suggested that the three girls go to the authorities and explain. She thought they might be able to keep Thera from being banished."

"Did they go to the authorities?" Beatrice asked when Primrose paused.

Primrose shook her head. "Nina was humiliated and frightened. She really was unaccustomed to magic, and facing witch police was just too much for her, so she fled back to the mortal world. And because she didn't stay to cooperate with the investigation, she was banished from the Sphere. Aura and Skye testified for Thera before the Witch Tribunal, but they couldn't save her."

"She *was* guilty, after all," Laurel burst out. "People seem to forget that and act like she was an innocent victim. I mean, she was there with all the illegal goods."

"That's right," Primrose said, "Thera probably *was* guilty."

"But she was taken away from her son," Beatrice said miserably. "What happened to Xan's father?"

"He came back and raised Xan after a fashion," Primrose said. "Actually, he wasn't a very good father. He died when Xan was ten or eleven, but Xan had really been on his own for a long time before that. And Aura went on to Witch U and then to work at the Witches' Institute. You know about her. She's quite successful, they say."

Beatrice nodded.

"As for Skye, she became bitter and didn't want anything to do with magic ever again. She left the witch academy and opened her shop. Eventually, she married Makepeace Drummond and they seem happy enough. But I know that she's never forgiven your mother," Primrose said sadly. "Aura, on the other hand, held herself responsible for not realizing that Nina would want to prove herself to her friends. Aura's always felt guilty."

"And my mother must feel guilty about Thera Renshaw," Beatrice said. *What a terrible thing to have to live with*, she thought.

"I'm sure she does," Primrose agreed. "Three young witches changed a lot of lives that day—because of ego and ambition. But you know, Beatrice, we all make mistakes. And I see in you," she added softly, "all the good your mother has done. She needs to forgive herself."

Beatrice nodded. Then her thoughts shifted back

to Xan, and she wondered if he would ever be able to forgive.

"Do you think Xan became a smuggler because of what happened to his mother?" Beatrice asked. "Or would he have followed his father's path anyway?"

"Xan Renshaw is nothing like his father," Primrose said with conviction. "People and their gossip! Xan is a smuggler, all right, but not for evil. He smuggles in Begones who have done no real harm to anyone so they can see their families. He brings together parents and children, husbands and wives. He's never told me why he does it, but I suspect it's because he knows better than most what it feels like to be separated from a loved one."

Beatrice looked sharply at Primrose. "Are you sure that's what he's doing?"

"I *know* it," Primrose said. "And so do other people in this village that I could name. They never speak of it, of course, because the authorities would banish Xan if they had any proof."

"But this is terrible!" Beatrice burst out. "He has such an evil reputation."

"It's that reputation that protects him," Primrose said calmly. "As long as Dally Rumpe and other evildoers think Xan is working on the side of dark magic, they'll leave him alone."

Beatrice lay awake a long time after going to bed. She closed her eyes and tried not to think, but it didn't work.

Her mind continued to replay what her great-aunt had told her, over and over. *At least now,* Beatrice thought, *I know why Xan doesn't like me. And why Skye is so cold. And why my mother never told me about coming to the Witches' Sphere.*

It was a relief when Teddy's voice broke into Beatrice's obsessive thoughts.

"I've been listening to you toss and turn," Teddy said. "Are you okay?"

"I'm all right," Beatrice said. "I've been thinking how so many things make sense now. And I've just come up with a new one."

"What?"

"Why Dr. Featherstone wants to help me," Beatrice said. "It's because she couldn't help my mother."

13

More Secrets

On their way to lunch the next day, Teddy was wondering aloud if they would ever hear from the Witches' Executive Committee.

"Why bring us to the Sphere at all," Teddy complained, "if they aren't going to send us to Werewolf Close?"

Beatrice had been thinking the same thing. "Maybe we're supposed to learn something before we go," she said, recalling her baffling conversation with Yorick Figlock—which still didn't make any sense to her. "Or they could be giving me time to get to know my family."

"How much time do they think you need?" Teddy asked with a touch of impatience.

"To be honest," Cyrus said, "I'm not sure I want to go back to the swamp. It was kind of—terrifying."

They had reached the front of the restaurant and Teddy yanked the door open, obviously annoyed. "Did you expect swamps and enchanted fog and werewolves *not* to be terrifying?" she demanded. "I hope you're not thinking of backing out now. Because I have a lot invested here."

"Me, me, me," Cyrus muttered as they went inside.

Beatrice saw Xan Renshaw getting up from a table and preparing to leave. "You guys go ahead and order," she said hastily. "I'll be right back."

She walked over to Xan's table, leaving her friends to stare after her. Xan saw her coming and eyed her suspiciously.

"What do you want?" he burst out, looking exasperated.

"I'm not stalking you, if that's what you think," Beatrice shot back, feeling a little put out herself. "I'd like to talk to you. *Outside*," she added, suddenly becoming aware of all the eyes focused on them.

Xan scowled, threw some bills on the table, and started for the door. Beatrice squared her shoulders, and ignoring the looks from the other diners, followed him outside.

He was walking so fast, Beatrice had to jog to keep up. "Give me two minutes," she said. "I know about your mother. I know *everything*."

Xan came to an abrupt stop. Beatrice hurried over to him.

"Aunt Primrose told me what my mother did," she said in a rush, "so I don't blame you for not wanting to have anything to do with me. But I know if my mother were here, she'd tell you how sorry she is. She'd be asking for your forgiveness. So that's what I'm doing now—"

"All *right*," Xan said gruffly. "You apologized for your mother and now everything's peachy." He turned away, and Beatrice caught his arm. He stared down at the hand gripping him, looking startled, and for a moment, uncertain.

"I don't expect us to become friends," Beatrice started.

"Good! Because that's not likely to happen."

"*But*," Beatrice went on resolutely, "my Aunt Primrose likes you—actually, she admires you—"

Xan's eyebrows lifted and he smirked at her. "And now you admire me, too?" he asked sarcastically.

"No," Beatrice said honestly. "I don't even know you. But I was thinking—"

"Let me tell you what *I* was thinking," he cut in, his eyes narrowed as he studied her. "First, I was thinking that you're a lot like your mother, coming to the Sphere to prove what a powerful witch you are. Second, I was thinking that all you'll end up doing is making trouble for people. And third, I was thinking that I don't want to be around when you do it."

Beatrice looked away. His words stung, even though she understood why he might assume that she was nothing more than an ambitious young witch out to make a name for herself.

"Look," she said sharply, "I'm not a powerful witch, and I never will be. I don't even *care* about being powerful. I'm here because it's written in *The Bailiwick Family History* that I have to try to break Dally Rumpe's spell and free Bromwich and his daughters. I'd rather not," she admitted. "I'm afraid of the swamps, and *terrified* of going to Werewolf Close. But Bromwich and his daughters are family, and I promised Rhona when the spell was broken on Winter Wood that I'd do what I could to help her father and sisters." Beatrice sighed. "I'm just an Everyday witch, and not a very brave one, at that."

Xan looked surprised. Then skeptical. Finally, he sighed and rubbed his face with both hands, as if he were very tired. When his eyes met hers again, they didn't look angry, just weary.

"You should go home," he said dully. "If it's true that you have no power, you don't stand a chance against Dally Rumpe."

"So I've been told," Beatrice said drily. "But I've made up my mind. I'm staying. I just wanted to tell you how sorry I am." And since there was nothing left to be said, she turned to go back inside.

"Hey!"

Beatrice stopped. Xan came to stand beside her.

"I think you're insane," he said bluntly. "But I'm not sure I agree that you aren't brave."

Now it was Beatrice's turn to be surprised.

"*Someone* needs to stand up to Dally Rumpe," Xan said, frowning. "But you're going to need help." Suddenly his mouth twisted into what Beatrice thought might be a smile, but his eyes looked fierce. "I don't suppose you'd want to join forces with an evil character like me, would you?"

Beatrice just stared at him. Was this a joke?

"Or you can try it on your own," he said. "But I don't think you're that stupid."

What an arrogant witch he is, Beatrice thought hotly. "You might want to think about brushing up on your social skills," she muttered.

"I'm usually much worse," Xan said, and now he was definitely smiling. "I guess you bring out the best in me."

"Aunt Primrose says you do good," Beatrice said grudgingly, "helping Begones come back to visit their families."

The smile vanished. "Don't ever repeat that," he said gruffly.

"*All right,* I won't. Just tell me how you can help us get into Werewolf Close and break the spell."

"I'm not sure I can," he said. "We might all end up on the werewolves' menu. But I know more than you do. Maybe enough to save your life."

"*What* do you know?" Beatrice demanded.

"I can't tell you now," he replied. "Meet me tonight, as soon as it's dark. I'll be waiting behind Merriwether House."

"And you'll tell us how to get inside the Close?" Beatrice prodded.

"I'll take you to someone who might be able to help."

Beatrice was having doubts. "And just where is this someone?"

"In the swamp," Xan said.

Beatrice's mind was whirling when she went back inside the restaurant. She was so preoccupied, she didn't hear Fillian calling her name until he was right beside her. He was holding a napkin, and Beatrice realized that he must have been having his lunch.

"I didn't see you," she said.

"You were otherwise occupied," Fillian answered. "When I saw you go after Renshaw, I almost followed you outside."

Beatrice was perplexed. "Why would you follow me?"

"To warn you." Now Fillian sounded worried. "I know your Aunt Primrose feels sorry for Xan Renshaw, but she should have cautioned you to stay away from him."

Beatrice was getting tired of everybody warning her about something or someone. "Thanks for the advice," she said stiffly, and left to join her friends.

Teddy and Ollie had reservations about putting their lives in Xan Renshaw's hands. Cyrus didn't want to go into the swamp at night with anyone.

"Why does it have to be after dark?" Cyrus asked.

"I assume he doesn't want anyone to see us," Beatrice answered.

"Right. He doesn't want witnesses when he leads us into the quicksand," Teddy said drily.

"Do you trust him, Beatrice?" Ollie asked.

"Maybe." That was the most Beatrice could honestly commit to. "But something tells me that Xan holds the key to breaking Dally Rumpe's spell. And I agree with him about one thing—I don't think we can do this alone."

The others were forced to agree.

That evening, as they were finishing dinner, Beatrice said casually, "I think I'll go to bed early and read for a while."

"Not until you've had dessert," Molly protested. "I've made dragonfly pudding."

Beatrice and her friends ate their dessert quickly, watching anxiously as dusk gathered outside the dining room window. By the time they climbed the stairs to their rooms, the sky was dark and stars were beginning to come out.

They arranged pillows in their beds so that anyone looking in to say good night would think they were asleep. Then Ollie and Cyrus crept across the hall to join Beatrice and Teddy.

Beatrice placed Cayenne in the pocket of her backpack and climbed through the window. The others followed. They descended the trellis as quietly as they could.

Xan was waiting at the edge of the garden, just as he had waited for Bing. That had been bothering Beatrice, she realized now.

"We saw Bing slip out of the house and leave with you the other night," she whispered to Xan. "Where did you take him?"

"I didn't exactly *take* him," Xan whispered back. "He's been spying on me for a long time, and when he figured out what I was doing, he wanted to help. I tried to discourage him, but he kept following me everywhere, and I decided he'd be safer if I let him go with me sometimes. At least I could keep an eye on him."

"You mean he helps you smuggle in the Begones?" Beatrice pressed, wanting to hear from Xan himself that this was what he was involved in and not the trafficking of illegal herbs.

"When it's low risk, yes," Xan answered. "If I think we're going to run into trouble, I don't let him come."

"But he's just a kid," Teddy said.

In the dim light, they could see Xan's shoulders lift in a shrug. "Young or not, he needs to feel useful."

Beatrice could understand how Xan might feel sympathetic to Bing—a little boy who had lost his parents and was thought by everyone to be evil.

"So where are you taking us?" she asked.

"If you keep asking questions, we won't be going anywhere," Xan said impatiently.

Beatrice bristled. She was searching for an appropriate and cutting response when she realized that Xan had already taken off through the bushes. Beatrice started after him—and walked into a tree. "You aren't being very helpful so far," she hissed, rubbing the bump on her forehead.

Xan led them through the woods to Will-o'-the-wisp Road and then to the wharf. They climbed into a small boat that was tied up at the pier and were soon heading at high speed across the river.

"The Shellycoats patrol the river at night," Xan said, "so keep your eyes open for their barge. They don't like anyone going toward Werewolf Close after dark."

"What would they do if they saw us?" Ollie asked.

"They might just send us back," Xan said. "Or they could lock us up overnight. It depends on their mood."

There was no sign of the Shellycoats, and before long, the boat reached the strip of beach where Fillian had docked the day before. They climbed out onto the sand and Xan lit a lantern. When Beatrice saw the small blue flame spring to life, she murmured, "That looks vaguely familiar."

Xan knew what she meant. "Some of the lights in the swamps are mine," he said, "but not all. I've seen them myself, and I have no idea who or what they are."

Nor did he seem to care especially. It seemed to

Beatrice that witches in Friar's Lantern enjoyed the mystery of their lights.

Xan started down the packed-earth trail into the swamp, walking quickly and confidently. He appeared to know his way around here.

After they had walked awhile, Beatrice said to Xan's back, "We're going to see Yorick Figlock, aren't we?"

"That crazy old witch?" Teddy burst out. "What help can he be?"

"He *didn't* appear to be all that—alert," Ollie said tactfully.

"Things aren't always what they seem to be," Xan replied. Beatrice thought he sounded suspiciously cheerful.

"You mean he's not really crazy?" Cyrus asked. "Then why pretend to be?"

"You'd have to ask him that," Xan said.

When they reached the cabin, they found Yorick sitting in a chair beside the hearth. An oil lamp on the mantle cast a small circle of light around him, leaving the rest of the room in shadow.

Xan extinguished his lantern and walked in. "Merry meet," he said to Yorick. "I hope we're not disturbing you."

The old witch looked up. "You're always welcome here," Yorick said.

Beatrice moved toward him. "Do you remember me?" she asked.

Amusement gleamed in Yorick's eyes. "You've been listening to the people who wonder if I have my wits about me, haven't you?" he said. "You are Beatrice Bailiwick. And unless I'm as addled as most folks claim, I expect Xan has brought you here to ask for my help."

Beatrice tried to assimilate *this* Yorick Figlock with the one she had met the day before. Tonight, he sounded perfectly rational. But then what was the meaning of all that babble about her needing a guide and needing courage?

"Yorick, you know that Beatrice and her friends are supposed to find a way into Werewolf Close," Xan said, "and they do need your help. I was hoping you would tell them your story."

The old witch looked around at each of their faces, his expression thoughtful. Finally he said, "If you trust these young witches, Xan, then so do I. Why don't you all sit down?"

They pulled up rough benches from the table and gathered close. Cayenne crawled out of the backpack and curled up in her mistress' lap. Beatrice didn't know what to expect, but her heart was beating fast. Did Yorick really know how to enter and leave Werewolf Close?

"After my parents died many years ago," Yorick told them, "I was alone. I didn't have any other family. Not here, at least. Most of my ancestors lived in the southern part of the kingdom of Bailiwick. They were there when Dally Rumpe cast his spell that split the kingdom apart, and they became his prisoners behind the enchanted fog. From the time I was a very young witch, I would lie in bed at night and imagine rescuing my family and bringing them to Friar's Lantern. Then last summer, I found a way into the Close."

Everyone was looking at the old man in astonishment.

"I did," Yorick said, grinning at their expressions. "I went there and my family hid me while I tried to get them out. The trouble is, I have thirty relatives living inside the

147

Close. I could never work out a plan to rescue that many people at once," he said sadly. "Then word reached Dally Rumpe that someone had gotten through his impenetrable fog. He didn't know who I was, or where I was hiding, but he had people searching for me. So I had to flee and leave my family behind."

Suddenly the big gray bird flew out of the corner and landed on Yorick's shoulder. The sound of wings flapping woke Cayenne. She opened one green-gold eye and kept it glued on Old Foxy.

"I don't think you should try to go there," Yorick said to Beatrice. "Odds are, you'll never get out alive."

"You did," she said.

"Barely," Yorick answered. He pointed to his scarred face and held out his crooked left arm. "The werewolves did so much damage to my legs, I can't take a step without feeling pain."

"Can you tell us how you managed to get in?" Ollie asked gently.

Yorick sighed heavily, then he said, "There are two obstacles to getting in or out—the fog and the werewolves. With luck, I managed to escape from the werewolves still alive, but you may not be so fortunate."

"My friend," Beatrice said, glancing at Teddy, "has a talent that may help us. She can detect anyone or anything that's spying on us or means us immediate harm."

Teddy tried to look humble, but she couldn't refrain from glowing.

"There's still the circle of fog that surrounds the Close," Yorick said. "It's three miles wide and there's no way to go over it. Once you've entered the fog, you become disoriented and lose all sense of direction. But," he added with a twinkle in his eye, "I found a way to stay on course."

Beatrice and her friends leaned toward him eagerly.

Yorick smiled fondly at the bird on his shoulder. "It wasn't due to any genius of mine; it was Old Foxy here who got me through. Some animals have a true and perfect sense of direction," he explained, "like the homing pigeon. It's magical. Even witches don't understand how it works."

"Old Foxy has it?" Beatrice asked.

"He does," Yorick replied, "and I found out about it completely by accident. One day we were deep in the swamp gathering herbs when a storm blew in. It was terrible. The rain was coming down so hard, I couldn't see where I was going. The water was rising all around me. I knew if I didn't make it out quickly, I would drown. Then Old Foxy flew away—I thought. But I could hear him calling to me, so I followed him. He kept crying out, and I kept following—until he brought me back to this cabin. Later, he led me through the fog to Werewolf Close."

Yorick reached into his pocket and brought out a fistful of seed. He held up a cupped hand to Old Foxy, who let out a loud squawk and began to peck at the seeds. "Xan Renshaw is one of the few witches I trust," Yorick said, "so I told him how Old Foxy had guided me through the fog. I'm too crippled to even try another trip to the Close, but Xan thought Old Foxy might help him get in. Then he could start bringing out my family a few at a time, and other people, too. But this stubborn old bird," Yorick said, his voice rough with tenderness, "won't work for anyone but me I guess."

"So he can't help us," Beatrice said, her shoulders sagging in disappointment.

"No," Xan said, "but your cat might."

"Cayenne?"

All eyes turned to the drowsy mop in Beatrice's lap. At the sound of her name, Cayenne sat up and yawned, then looked expectantly at Beatrice. When Beatrice wasn't forthcoming with so much as one kitty treat, Cayenne began to swat her plumed tail impatiently against Beatrice's leg.

"Every time I've seen you since you've come to Friar's Lantern, your cat has been with you," Xan said. "There seems to be a strong bond between the two of you."

Beatrice nodded.

"Except that Cayenne—" Ollie glanced apologetically at the cat "—isn't big on following orders."

"But she loves Beatrice," Teddy pointed out.

Beatrice was regarding Cayenne thoughtfully. "Do you think you would be able to do it, Cay? Could you lead us through the fog?"

The cat looked steadily at Beatrice, then responded with an emphatic meow.

"I guess that means yes," Ollie said, grinning.

"Since you spent so much time in Werewolf Close," Beatrice said to Yorick, "you must know where Innes is kept."

Yorick nodded. "It's a cottage just inside the ring of fog. I can draw you a map."

"Have you ever seen the manticore that guards her?" Ollie asked.

"No, but I've talked to people who've seen him,"

Yorick said. "His name is Allbones. They say he's a vicious beast. But not invincible," Yorick added with a faint smile.

"What do you mean?" Beatrice asked.

"I've been told that if you can face the manticore without fear, he becomes powerless and can't harm you. But you can't just act unafraid," Yorick said. "It must be genuine fearlessness for Allbones to lose his power over you. And that requires true courage. Didn't I tell you?" he said softly to Beatrice. "You need two things . . . "

"A guide," Beatrice said, beginning to smile, "and courage. So that's what you meant. But why were you talking in riddles?"

Yorick frowned. "You were here with Fillian Hawthorn."

"So?"

Yorick made an impatient motion with his good hand. "That witch? I'm not sure I trust him at all."

"So you aren't really crazy," Cyrus said bluntly.

Yorick grinned. "No more than any of the other loony witches running loose in Friar's Lantern." Then he grew thoughtful. "But just in case the stories about me going to Werewolf Close ever reach Dally Rumpe's ears, I figure it's best if folks think I'm missing some of my buttons. I mean, how much of a threat can a crazy old witch be?"

As they were walking back to the boat, Ollie said, "Well, at least we know more going into Werewolf Close than we did about Winter Wood."

"But you don't know the swamps," Xan said over his shoulder. "That's why I need to go with you."

Beatrice felt a rush of gratitude, but she remembered quickly that this was her fight, not his. And why would he risk his life to help the daughter of Nina Merriwether, anyway?

"We can't ask you to do that," she said.

"I don't remember you asking," he replied.

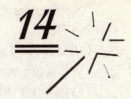

14

A Change of Plans

The next morning, when she was sure they had the house to themselves, Beatrice spread out the map Yorick had drawn for them on the dining room table. Teddy and Cyrus leaned close to look at it. Ollie was sitting nearby with his face buried in a thick book.

"Okay," Beatrice said, blowing her bangs aside, "Innes's cottage is *here*—so if we approach Werewolf Close from Yorick's cabin, we'll be fairly close to her."

"Only three miles of fog separating us," Cyrus said drily.

"What about the Witches' Executive Committee?" Teddy said suddenly. "We're making all these plans and they may never tell us to go."

"I guess if we haven't heard from them in a couple of days," Beatrice replied thoughtfully, "we go on our own."

Teddy looked at her in surprise.

"They didn't give us any useful advice last time," Cyrus pointed out. "And now we have Xan to help us."

"Do we?" Teddy asked. "I'm still not sure we can trust him."

"Neither am I," Beatrice admitted. "What do you think, Ollie?"

Ollie looked up. "What? Did you say something?"

"What are you doing over there?" Teddy asked.

"I've been looking through some of Primrose and Laurel's books," Ollie said. He got up and went over to join them, bringing the book he had been reading with him. "I was trying to find a spell or a talisman or something to protect us in the fog and once we're in Werewolf Close."

"Have you found anything?" Beatrice asked.

"Not yet. This book is really old and I don't understand most of what I'm reading," Ollie admitted ruefully. "Maybe I should go to the library and check out *Spells for Dummies*."

"I'd forget the spells, if I were you," Teddy said sagely. "Speaking from personal experience, they're never as easy as they sound."

Just then, Laurel came barreling through the front door. She was obviously in an agitated state.

"I'm glad I found all of you together," she said, eyes blazing as she rushed into the dining room. "I just heard that you've been hanging around that awful Xan Renshaw. What do you think you're doing?" she demanded. "Didn't I warn you about him?"

"Boy, word sure gets around fast in this place," Cyrus murmured.

"Who told you we were with Xan?" Beatrice asked.

"That isn't important," Laurel replied. Then she said, "Oh, I don't suppose it matters. Fillian told me."

"I see," Beatrice said.

"But don't get me off track," Laurel chided her. "You're

154

not to have anything more to do with that criminal. Do you understand?"

"We understand what you're saying, Aunt Laurel," Beatrice answered.

"All right then," Laurel said, calming down a little. "Oh—and I have Teddy and Cyrus's hats ready. Why don't you come by the shop this morning for a fitting?"

Teddy's face lit up. "Great! We'll be there."

"Yeah . . . great," Cyrus said with a noticeable lack of enthusiasm.

After Laurel was gone, Beatrice said, "That Fillian Hawthorn is starting to get on my nerves."

"He's awfully good looking," Teddy said slowly, "not to mention, being Classical. But he shouldn't have tattled to your Aunt Laurel."

"Maybe he's just trying to look out for us," Cyrus suggested.

"Or maybe he has motives we don't know about for wanting to keep us out of Werewolf Close," Ollie said darkly.

Teddy's eyes twinkled as she looked at Ollie. "That couldn't be jealousy I hear, could it?"

"I don't know what you're talking about," Ollie muttered, and started thumbing through his book.

"Well, Fillian *has* been paying a lot of attention to Beatrice," Teddy pointed out wickedly. "And he's smart, and good looking, and—"

"He does seem too good to be true, doesn't he?" Ollie said with a touch of sarcasm.

"Teddy, please stop it," Beatrice demanded, looking embarrassed and annoyed.

"Yeah, Teddy," Cyrus said. "We've got serious business going on here."

"You're right," Teddy said brightly. "We have hats to try on."

Cyrus groaned.

"Ollie, why don't you and I go to the library and research protective talismans," Beatrice said, "while Teddy and Cyrus have their fittings?"

"We'll meet you at The Cat and the Fiddle for lunch," Teddy said. "*I'll* be the one in the dazzling Laurel Merriwether original."

"*I'll* be the one hiding under the table," Cyrus added.

Friar's Lantern Public Library was an ancient brick building next door to the witch academy. Bookshelves filled with dusty volumes that appeared very old and scholarly rose up to the vaulted ceiling. When Beatrice, Ollie, and Cayenne walked in, the first thing they noticed was a young witch suspended in the air above their heads. She was replacing books on a high shelf.

"Merry meet," the witch called out cheerfully. "I'll be right down."

She seemed to be coming in for a perfect landing, but at a high rate of speed.

"Oh, dear," the witch squeaked, right before she crashed into the checkout desk. The books in her arms went flying, and one heavy tome fell squarely on her head.

Beatrice winced.

The witch stood up, appearing a little shaky, and straightened her crimson robes in a delayed attempt at dignity. She smoothed her long black hair, adjusted her pointed hat, and came to meet Beatrice and Ollie. A very large white cat came with her.

"I'm Juliana Bright," the witch said, sounding as perky as her name, "and this is my assistant Ulysses. How may we help you?"

"We want to research talismans," Ollie said. He was looking around at all the books with a blissful expression.

"What kind of talisman, specifically? For health? Air travel? Riot control?" Juliana Bright reeled them off methodically.

"No, for protection," Beatrice said.

"Ah, that's an easy one," the librarian said. She stared up at one of the top shelves and a thick brown book came sailing down into her hands. She flipped through the pages efficiently and then stopped. "Here we are. Protection rites, rituals, and compounds, pages 126 through 284. This book can't be removed from the library," she told them, "but you can sit down at one of the tables and copy what you need."

"Do you have a photocopier?" Ollie asked her.

Juliana Bright gasped. "Brimstone and broomsticks!" she exclaimed with indignation. "No, we do not have a photocopier. These are *rare* volumes. Photocopiers would damage them."

"Sorry," Ollie said.

Juliana Bright walked off mumbling, "*Do we have a photocopier* . . . Next they'll be asking for an ancient spells database!"

Beatrice and Ollie sat down at a long table where there were quilled pens, inkwells, and stacks of scrap parchment. Ollie opened the book to page 126, and they started to read. A while later, Beatrice said, "All this sounds pretty complicated."

"It does," Ollie agreed, looking disappointed.

Beatrice's eyes moved down the page—and then something caught her eye. "Hey, this sounds easy. 'Herbal mixtures to aid in countermagic and protection,'" she read. "All you have to do is pulverize the herbs, steep them in water for twenty-four hours, pour off the water, stick them in a bag, and carry the bag with you."

"We can probably get the herbs at Beyond Thyme," Ollie said, brightening up, "and have them ready in a couple of days."

Beatrice reached for a quill and dipped it into an inkwell.

A few minutes later, Ollie was reciting the list of herbal ingredients and Beatrice was scribbling away when a shadow fell across the book. Beatrice and Ollie looked up to see Fillian Hawthorn standing over them.

"What a surprise," Fillian said, smiling. He peered at the open book. "Ahhh, countermagic and protection. This is fairly advanced, you know."

"It makes sense to me," Beatrice answered, an obstinate note creeping into her voice. "So it can't be all *that* advanced."

"Hmmm . . . Yes . . . But magic can be trickier than it first appears," Fillian said, looking steadily at her. "I hope you aren't studying up on spells to help you in Werewolf Close. That would be a big mistake. Magic by the numbers won't do it with someone as powerful as Dally Rumpe."

Beatrice sat there looking pleasant and mentally tapping her foot with impatience.

"Well . . ." Fillian said into the silence, "I won't keep you from your work. Good luck with *whatever* it is you're doing."

Ollie stared hard at Fillian's back as he walked away. "See what a snoop he is?" Ollie demanded. "That witch is *determined* to keep us out of Werewolf Close."

After they had finished writing down the compounding formula, Beatrice and Ollie headed for Beyond Thyme. Magnus Pinch was behind the counter filling an apothecary jar with something pink and oozy. When Beatrice saw it, rat intestines came to mind and she felt profoundly queasy. Magnus had looked up when the bell over the door jingled, and now he quickly slipped the jar under the counter. Beatrice wondered if the pink stuff was one of his secret formulas.

"Merry meet," she greeted him, and held out the list of ingredients they would need. "Can you fill this order?"

Magnus Pinch's eyes traveled down the list. "Juniper, myrrh, madwort, hellebore . . ." He looked up with a small knowing smile. "You're making a protective talisman. And would that be something you'll use in Werewolf Close?"

Ignoring his question, Ollie asked, "Do you have everything on the list?"

The herbalist's smile evaporated. "Certainly," he snapped. "These are frightfully common herbs, you know, and not likely to provide much protection at all."

Magnus began to take down bottles from the shelves behind him and measure out the herbs into small bags. "Did Yorick Figlock give you the formula when you were there?" he asked slyly while he worked. "Or was it Skye Drummond when you stopped by her shop?"

"You seem to have been keeping tabs on us," Beatrice said, frowning.

Magnus glanced up at her and smirked. "Your every move is followed by eyes all over the village," he said. "You probably don't know this, but even though Yorick and Skye are Classical, they know nothing about the more—shall we say, *esoteric* herbs. Now I could fix you up with something very powerful," he added with a cunning gleam in his eyes, "using herbs not readily available in these parts."

Beatrice glanced at Ollie and she knew they were wondering the same thing: Could Magnus be receiving illegal herbs, or perhaps, smuggling them in himself?

It was almost lunchtime when Beatrice and Ollie left the herb shop. On their way to The Cat and the Fiddle, Beatrice noticed Skye Drummond standing in the doorway of her shop, watching them. Beatrice raised her hand in greeting, and Skye stepped back inside, swiftly closing the door behind her.

When Beatrice and Ollie entered the restaurant, they saw Teddy and Cyrus seated at a table in the center of the dining room. *That would be Teddy's doing*, Beatrice thought with a grin, *not wanting anyone to miss her new hat.*

As if anyone could. It was a witch's hat made of bright red satin. Laurel had draped black netting around the crown and showered it with an abundance of silver stars that glittered when Teddy moved her head.

Cyrus's hat was still in its box, tucked away discreetly at his feet. As Beatrice and Ollie approached the table, Beatrice noticed that Cyrus kept glancing covertly at Teddy's hat, looking as if he'd like to be any place except where he was.

"Well?" Teddy demanded as Beatrice and Ollie sat down, turning her head first one way, then the other. "What do you think?"

Ollie appeared to be overwhelmed.

"It's—*amazing*," Beatrice said, thinking that Laurel had certainly made a hat that was unique and dramatic. Just like Teddy. "It suits you," Beatrice added honestly.

Teddy beamed. "I thought so, too."

While they were having lunch, Xan came in. He walked over to their table, did a double take when he saw Teddy's hat, and then said softly, "We should leave tonight. There's going to be a full moon and we won't have to use a lantern until we enter the swamp."

Beatrice and her friends were startled by this news.

"So soon?" Beatrice whispered back.

"The sooner the better, before anyone catches on to what we're doing," Xan told her. "Meet me at the pier after dark."

Xan left and went to sit down at a table across the room. He didn't look their way again.

"Does it seem to you that he's awfully eager?" Teddy

asked. "And we still haven't heard from the Executive Committee."

"If we succeed in breaking the spell, the committee probably won't care that we didn't wait," Beatrice reasoned. "And if we fail, they won't classify us Classical anyway."

"Good point," Ollie said. "But we won't have time to do anything with the herbs. We'll just have to depend on Teddy to get us past the werewolves."

Teddy frowned. "I'd feel a lot better if we had a Plan B."

Beatrice made the announcement at dinner.

"What do you mean you're leaving tonight?" Primrose bellowed. "You haven't heard from the committee."

"And taking Xan Renshaw," Laurel said with real alarm in her voice. "Have you people lost your minds?"

"You have to wait for instructions," Primrose declared.

"You *can't* go with that smuggler," Laurel insisted.

Molly was watching them all calmly. "Miss Primrose," she said, "you knew they'd be going to the Close sooner or later."

"Then let it be later," Primrose snapped.

"And not with Xan Renshaw," Laurel added.

"If anyone can get them through those swamps, Xan can," Primrose said testily.

"I'd better go upstairs and read through the spell I have to recite," Beatrice told them.

"It's nearly dark," Ollie said. "We should all be getting ready."

As they left the table, Primrose exchanged a look of frustration with Laurel. "This isn't turning out the way we planned at all," Primrose grumbled.

15

Into the Fog

Xan was waiting for them on the pier. Still muttering the spell she would need to recite when they found Innes, Beatrice climbed into the boat after Teddy. Her foot struck a large lump and she heard a muffled "Ow!"

Xan leaned down to investigate. When he pulled back a piece of canvas, they saw that the lump was Bing.

"What do you think you're doing?" Xan said to the boy.

"Coming with you," Bing answered.

"Not on this trip you're not."

"That's not fair," Bing protested. "You've let me go before."

"Not to Werewolf Close I haven't."

"I don't have to go all the way inside," Bing said, his voice taking on a pleading tone. "Just across the river. Then I'll come straight back."

"Bing, it's too dangerous," Xan said wearily.

"Please?" came the boy's small voice.

Beatrice was surprised to hear Bing asking and not demanding. And politely, too. Perhaps that was what swayed Xan. "All right," he said, "you can ride in the boat with us, and I'll take you to Yorick Figlock. He'll see that you get home."

They were nearly halfway across the river when Ollie said, "Xan, there's a raft or something coming downriver. It doesn't have any lights and I can't see who's on it."

"It's the Shellycoats' barge," Xan said.

"Uh-oh," Ollie said. "It looks like they're coming straight for us."

The barge was no more than a shadow against the dark water, but Beatrice could tell that it was definitely heading in their direction. If the Shellycoats hadn't already seen them, they soon would.

"Our boat can move faster than the barge," Xan said in a low voice. "Maybe we can slip past."

Then he mumbled something, and the boat sped up. Beatrice and her friends crouched down, scarcely breathing, with their eyes glued to the barge.

"The tricky part will be when we reach shore," Xan murmured. "They'll be able to see us for sure on the white sand. And by the time we're all out of the boat, they'll be on top of us."

"We're almost there now," Beatrice said. "What do we do?"

"I guess we hope they turn around in the next two minutes," Xan answered.

The boat was just a few yards off shore when Beatrice felt a gentle rocking, and she realized that Bing was getting to his feet. He swung his arm wide and threw something far out into the water. A second later there was the sound of a splash that carried over the silent river. The

Shellycoats must have heard it because almost instantly the barge slowed down and then started back upriver in the direction of the splash.

"Bing, that was quick thinking," Xan said. "What was it you threw?"

"A stone I picked up while I was waiting for you," the boy answered, sounding pleased with himself.

"You're a hero, Bing," Beatrice said. "Thank you."

"Any time," Bing replied cheerfully.

"The Shellycoats could still come back," Xan said as the boat slid up on the beach. "Everybody out—quickly. I'll hide the boat in these bushes."

They were running across the sand toward the swamp when Beatrice thought she heard someone singing. She stopped and stood very still, listening. It was definitely a woman singing in a high clear voice. Beatrice looked back at the river and saw a tiny figure in white perched on an island of rocks just offshore. Long golden hair gleamed in the moonlight.

"It's Trill!" Beatrice exclaimed. "The river nymph."

"We don't have time for river nymphs," Cyrus said scornfully. "Come on, Beatrice."

But Beatrice didn't move. She had caught a few words of the song and wanted to hear more. The others looked back to see what was keeping her.

"Hey," Ollie said softly. "I think that song's about us."

No one spoke as they strained to hear what Trill was singing.

Have you heard of them, the fearless four?
Listen now and you'll hear still more.

For they've come back on their noble quest,
They'll not give up, nor will they rest,
    Till they've seen it through.

Each with a gift that they will share,
They can do together, with astounding flair,
What wouldn't be possible on their own.
They'll stand together, never alone,
    Till they've seen it through.

"What's their secret?" you may ask,
What magic do they bring to the task?
It's friendship, not the might of the foe,
That can tip the scales and strike a blow—
    Till they've seen it through.

When the song ended, Ollie said, "I think that river nymph was telling us we can do this."

"Well, we succeeded in Winter Wood," Cyrus said doubtfully, "but I'm still not sure how we did it."

Neither was Beatrice, but she was grateful for the river nymph's vote of confidence. "Thank you, Trill," Beatrice called out softly.

They were starting toward the swamp when a robed man carrying a lantern suddenly emerged from the trees. It was Yorick Figlock, leaning on a crutch and moving slowly.

"Merry meet and welcome," he greeted them.

"Yorick, I didn't expect you to be here," Xan said.

"I came to wish you well," the old witch said, "and to give each of you something to take on your journey."

He reached inside his robes and withdrew a leather

pouch. They all watched as he loosened the strings and poured out what looked like several smooth pebbles into the palm of his hand.

"These are amulets," Yorick said, giving everyone a stone. "They will bring you good fortune, and more important," he added, looking straight into Beatrice's eyes, "they will give you courage."

"To fight the manticore," Beatrice murmured, studying the stone in her hand. It was the color of dark wood smoke, and when she held it up to the light, she saw that it was shot with veins of silver and gold. Beatrice squeezed the amulet tightly for a moment, then slipped it into the pocket of her jeans.

"Yorick, can Bing stay with you until we get back?" Xan asked.

"Certainly."

"And if we haven't returned by morning," Xan said, "will you take him to Merriwether House?"

"I should go with you!" Bing burst out. "I saved you from the Shellycoats, didn't I?"

"Indeed you did," Xan said gravely. "But you can help me now by staying with Yorick."

Just then, a gust of wind swept through the swamp, causing the hanging moss to dance fitfully.

"Do you think a storm's coming?" Xan asked Yorick.

The old witch raised his face to the sky. "Not a cloud in sight," he said. "Just the moon and the stars."

The wind was picking up now, blustering its way through the swamp and whipping at their clothes and hair. Beatrice and her friends huddled together, blinking against the sand and leaves being kicked up in their faces.

"What's that noise?" Teddy shouted.

Beatrice heard what she thought was the wind whistling through the trees; then she realized that it sounded more like a howl then a whistle.

Suddenly Beatrice sensed that they weren't alone. She raised her head slowly, narrowing her eyes against the blasts of air still striking her in the face. And then she saw them. Weaving in and out among the trees were the white translucent forms of ghosts. *Dozens* of ghosts. They all seemed to be floating toward the beach, moaning and howling in a most disconcerting way.

"We have visitors!" Beatrice yelled.

"Galloping gremlins!" Bing blurted out, and buried his face in Xan's side.

"Don't be afraid!" Yorick shouted. "It's only the spirits of the swamp. They've come to say that they know why you're here and are happy to see you."

"You could have fooled me!" Cyrus exclaimed.

The ghosts floated at the edge of the swamp for a few moments and then started to retreat back into the trees. Immediately, the wind began to die down and the howling grew softer, until finally, there was only stillness and quiet.

Beatrice let out the breath she had been holding and the others glanced at each other and smirked.

"I don't think this amulet worked for me," Teddy said with a nervous giggle. "I'm a wreck."

"It will work when you need it," Yorick told her. Then he said to Xan, "You should be leaving now. I'll take the boy home with me."

"We'll walk with you as far as your cabin," Xan said.

"No, I'll just slow you down. Merry part to you all until we meet again."

Even at night they could see the fog billowing over the trees. Xan led them steadily toward it, until finally, they emerged from the darkness into a moonlit clearing. Some fifty yards away, the wall of dense whirling vapor rose up to meet the sky.

Beatrice slipped a harness over Cayenne's head, buckled it, and attached the leash. Cayenne expressed her displeasure by switching her tail rapidly back and forth.

"I know you don't like it," Beatrice said, "but I have to hold onto you."

The air around them was suffocatingly hot and wet. A sense of dread settled over Beatrice as she imagined walking into that sultry and blinding mist. Teddy, Ollie, and Cyrus were standing close together and staring into the fog with obvious trepidation.

"I keep thinking about the werewolves," Teddy said. "Assuming I can locate them, how do we get away? You know we can't run as fast as a werewolf."

"Perhaps I can help you," came a voice from the swamp.

They all turned to see who had spoken. There was a rustling of leaves, a quivering of underbrush, and then Longshank, the water leaper, emerged into the clearing.

His ugly little face glistened wetly in the moonlight as

he looked up at them. "Good evening to you all," he said politely.

"Hello, Longshank," Beatrice said. She doubted seriously that this little creature could help them outrun werewolves, but she was glad to see him just the same.

"I understand that the cat will lead you through the fog and keep you on course," Longshank said. "I wouldn't be able to do that, but I can move faster than a werewolf."

"Only we're too big to ride on your back," Beatrice said. Then suddenly the solution came to her, and she burst out, "Cyrus's shrinking spell!"

"Exactly," Longshank replied. "Trill, the river nymph, sang a song about your magic one day, and as soon as I heard that one of you can cast a shrinking spell, the idea began to form in my mind."

"I can shrink us as small as three inches," Cyrus told Beatrice. "For some reason, I've never been able to go smaller."

"Three inches," Longshank murmured. "I could probably carry three of you—plus the cat, of course."

"Only three?" Ollie asked. "But there are five of us, including Xan."

"I wish I could take all five," Longshank said, "but I can't carry too much weight and still outleap the werewolves."

"Then we need to decide who will go," Beatrice said. "I'll have to be there to recite the counterspell, and Teddy will need to go to warn us when a werewolf is approaching."

"I have to shrink you," Cyrus pointed out.

"You'll do that before we enter the fog," Beatrice said thoughtfully. "We'll be coming in near Innes's cottage, so we won't have to travel very far inside the Close. It probably wouldn't matter if we stayed small—in fact, it might be a good idea; we'd be less conspicuous."

"Do you think we'll need Ollie's boiling water spell?" Teddy asked.

"I don't know," Beatrice said. "Maybe."

"Don't forget my knowledge of the swamps," Xan reminded her.

"But you don't know Werewolf Close," Beatrice pointed out. "As much as I'd like to have you with us, Xan, if we can only take three . . ."

"I understand," Xan said quietly.

There was a brief silence, and then Cyrus said with obvious reluctance, "I got to go inside Winter Wood. So if you don't think you'll need me this time, it's only fair that Ollie should be the one to go."

"That's really decent of you, Cyrus," Ollie said.

"I just thought of something," Beatrice said. "How can Cayenne lead us if she's riding on Longshank's back?"

Longshank leaped over to Cayenne. He looked into her face and made a deep rumbling sound in his throat. Cayenne responded with a series of sharp meows.

Longshank turned to Beatrice. "Your cat says that she can communicate directions to me. She'll tell me when to leap left and when to leap right, when to speed up and when to slow down. It just might work. She's a very articulate cat—but I'm sure you already know that."

"All right then," Xan said. "If there's nothing else to talk about, you'd best be on your way."

"Stand close together, so I can touch all of you," Cyrus told them. "Beatrice, can you hold Cayenne?" Then he began to chant:

> By the mysteries, one and all,
> Make them shrink from tall to small.
> Cut them down to inches three,
> As my will, so mote it be.

In a flash, Beatrice, Teddy, Ollie, and Cayenne shrank smaller and smaller, until they barely came up to Cyrus's ankle.

"What an amazing spell!" Xan exclaimed.

"You should be on this end of it," Teddy grumbled. "I feel really dizzy."

"All right," Longshank said brightly. "All passengers for Werewolf Close, hop aboard!"

Beatrice climbed on the water leaper's back and Cayenne leaped up in front of her.

"Grab the loose skin at the back of my neck," Longshank said.

Beatrice hesitated. "Won't that hurt you?"

"Don't worry, I'm tough."

Beatrice looped Cayenne's leash around her wrist and gripped the back of Longshank's neck. Teddy and Ollie climbed up behind her.

"Put your arms around my waist," Beatrice told Teddy. "Ollie, you hold onto Teddy."

"Safe journey," Xan said to them.

"I'll be waiting for you," Cyrus added, sounding forlorn.

"We'll see you soon," Beatrice said, trying to sound confident.

Then Longshank took off with a six-foot leap. The next jump was closer to seven feet. Before she knew it, Beatrice felt the fog wrap around her like wet gauze. Even though it was intensely hot, a shiver ran down Beatrice's spine and goose bumps popped up on her arms. She couldn't see anything but darkness. And the only thing she could hear was Cayenne's occasional meow as the cat gave Longshank directions.

The water leaper was moving at an astounding speed. As the minutes passed, Beatrice began to feel more confident. How could a werewolf possibly catch them going this fast? Then she thought she heard a sound behind them. Very *close* behind them.

"Teddy," Beatrice said sharply. "Do your spell!"

Teddy started chanting:

> *Candle, bell, and willow tree,*
> *Who does stalk and spy on me?*
> *With your magic and your charm,*
> *Show us who would do us harm.*

Suddenly, there was a flash in the darkness. Beatrice looked over her shoulder and saw a pool of light only inches away from the water leaper's outstretched leg. What was revealed by the light made Beatrice gasp.

She was staring into the glittering yellow eyes of a snarling werewolf. Beatrice had the fleeting impression of gaping jaws and bared fangs, of hot breath scalding the side of her face and neck. Then she screamed.

16

Werewolf Close

Cayenne emitted a sharp, "*Meow.*" Longshank instantly leaped to the right and sped up. The werewolf dropped back, and the pool of light vanished.

"Just keep saying the spell, Teddy!" Beatrice called over her shoulder.

Teddy repeated the spell several times and no light appeared. Then suddenly there was another flash and Beatrice saw a vicious hairy face to their right. Cayenne cried out and Longshank leaped to the left, leaving the werewolf behind.

Teddy's frenzied mutterings and Cayenne's rapid-fire meows filled the void around them as they raced through the darkness. *Surely we must be getting close*, Beatrice thought, fervently hoping that her cat did have a magical sense of direction.

Suddenly there was a flash of light behind them, then one to the left of Longshank's shoulder, and one to the right and slightly ahead of them. Beatrice was stunned by the realization that they were surrounded by werewolves. There was no place for them to go!

Cayenne must have been communicating that fact to Longshank with her frantic cries because the water leaper kept speeding straight ahead without veering from his course—as the werewolves on either side of them moved closer.

Beatrice didn't know what to do. It looked like there was no way out. In desperation, she began to chant:

> *Circle of magic, hear my plea,*
> *Drop hailstones large*
> *On our enemy.*
> *This, I ask you, do for me.*

All at once, a flurry of hailstones the size of melons plummeted down into the pools of light, clobbering the werewolves on their long fanged muzzles and bony skulls. The horrible creatures howled in pain and fury, then turned and ran to escape the icy assault.

A few moments later, the fog began to thin. Beatrice could see watery light just ahead, and a wave of heat struck her in the face. Longshank made two great leaps and they emerged from the fog into the brilliance of Werewolf Close.

They found themselves at the edge of a shallow pond of stagnant water. The sun burned fiercely through a spotty grove of stunted and dying trees, searing their flesh with its malevolent rays. Beatrice slid off Longshank's back and led Cayenne to a shady spot under a bush. The others followed.

Panting and exhausted, Longshank collapsed on the brown brittle grass. Beatrice wiped his wet face with her shirttail.

"You were so fast and so brave," she told him. "We never could have done it without you. And without Teddy and Cayenne," she added, beaming at the two of them.

Longshank grinned weakly, Cayenne purred, and Teddy's eyes sparkled. The terrible heat had sapped Beatrice's strength and she sat down heavily beside the water leaper.

Ollie was lying on his belly peering around. "It's so quiet. I don't see any people, but there are some houses over there." He was looking at a cluster of weathered cabins with sagging roofs and rickety porches overgrown with weeds.

"Everybody probably stays inside," Teddy said, wiping the sweat from her face with the back of her hand. "Out of this awful sun."

"Look!" Beatrice said suddenly. "That must be Innes's cottage—just where Yorick said it would be."

A low white house with a small courtyard in front stood just beyond the cabins. A ring of dead trees surrounded the cottage, their leafless branches intertwined protectively over the red tile roof.

"Wait for us here," Beatrice said to Longshank.

"Oh, no," he protested, struggling to stand. "You can't go alone. You might need me."

"We need you to rest," Beatrice said gently, "and be ready to help us escape if we have to. You couldn't do that as weak as you are now."

"I suppose that's true," Longshank admitted reluctantly. "But call my name if you run into trouble. I'll be there in two shakes of a water leaper's webbed foot. Do you want to leave Cayenne with me?" he added. "I'd be honored to keep company with such a gifted cat."

"Thanks, Longshank."

After stroking Cayenne and handing the leash to the water leaper, Beatrice looked at Teddy and Ollie.

"Ready to go?" she asked.

Ollie took a deep breath and nodded. "As ready as I'll ever be," he said.

Beatrice, Teddy, and Ollie started toward the white house. Still only three inches tall, they found some relief from the blazing sun by walking in the shade of the dead brush that edged the pool.

Beatrice noticed that no crops or flowers grew in Werewolf Close. There were only barren fields of cracked brown earth spreading out around them. A film of dust had settled over the dead and dying trees and the few plants that struggled to live in this parched corner of the Witches' Sphere. A man in ragged robes was stretched out in a hammock beside one of the cabins. He appeared too weary to even shoo away the flies that buzzed around his listless face.

They had come about halfway around the pond when Beatrice noticed movement in the water out of the corner of her eye. She turned and saw a long winding ripple in the pool's surface a few feet away. At the end of the ripple, just above the water, was the large triangular head of a snake. It had to be at least three feet long, and was headed in their direction.

Beatrice shouted, "Look out!"

"*What?*" a startled Teddy demanded. Then she saw the snake. As did Ollie.

"Let's get out of here!" Ollie yelled.

"And go where?" Teddy was looking around frantically. "There's nothing to climb. And we're so small, and it's so big—"

The snake had reached the edge of the pond, its hooded eyes glinting in the burning sun. In another moment, the reptile's venomous head would be out of the water.

Suddenly Ollie began to chant:

> *Heat of flame, heat of fire,*
> *Give to me my one desire.*
> *Boil this water, bubbling free,*
> *As my will, so mote it be!*

Instantly, the water in the pond began to bubble. The snake jerked, then turned sharply and started to glide toward the opposite bank.

Beatrice was trembling. "Good move, Ollie," she said in a weak voice.

"No one said *anything* about snakes," Teddy pointed out indignantly. "You'd think they would have at least mentioned the possibility."

They continued on with greater caution around the pond and past the cabins. Innes's cottage was only a few yards away. They could see through lacy wrought-iron gates into the courtyard. And what they saw made their hearts start to pound.

There sat Allbones, the manticore. He was at least seven feet tall and thin to the point of gauntness, his long bones jutting out beneath the loose skin of a lion's pelt. He had the tail and shaggy mane of a lion, but his face could have been that of a human—*almost*, Beatrice thought, because it was so pale and waxy it seemed drained of all blood. And the yellow six-inch fangs and twisted horns protruding from his forehead could have only belonged to a monster.

Beatrice, Teddy, and Ollie crept behind a pile of rocks, where they could watch Allbones without being seen. The creature was sitting on the ground with his long hind legs stretched out in front of him. He was chuckling—a cold mirthless sound that chilled Beatrice to the marrow—as he peered at the collection of objects spread out around him. Beatrice looked closer and realized that they were lanterns.

Suddenly Allbones looked up, instantly alert, as if he had heard something. His eyes glowed red as they moved over the landscape. Beatrice, Teddy, and Ollie crouched lower behind the rocks. They watched in horrified fascination as a dozen tiny creatures came running from behind the house toward the manticore.

Beatrice recoiled at the sight of their gray pointed faces covered with knotty warts, at the long strands of hair sprouting from the tops of their skull-like heads, at the skinny gray arms and legs poking through the greasy rags they wore. She wasn't certain what these monstrosities were, but she imagined they were some kind of evil imp.

Allbones was glaring at the imps as they gathered around him. "You were supposed to be here an hour ago," the manticore said.

Beatrice, Teddy, and Ollie could understand him perfectly, even though he didn't exactly speak in words. As Dr. Meadowmouse had said, the monster's voice sounded like the tones of a musical instrument, resulting in something very close to normal speech but not quite. There was an echo after each word that had an unpleasant metallic ring.

"Well, don't just stand there," Allbones said harshly to the imps. "You're to search across the river this time, and their night will be ending soon. Our master, Dally Rumpe, has long since grown impatient with your failure to find the gold." The manticore's red eyes glittered alarmingly. "He won't tolerate your incompetence forever."

The imps were chattering among themselves like little monkeys, seeming oblivious to the manticore's warning.

"And make sure they see your lights from the village," Allbones continued. "Dally Rumpe will be displeased if you don't frighten at least a few of those witless witches tonight."

Ollie glanced at Beatrice. "Now we know who's behind the lights in the swamp," he whispered. "It must be Innes's gold they're searching for."

"And at the same time, Dally Rumpe can get a kick out of scaring the village witches," Teddy added.

"Well, the joke's on him," Beatrice said, smiling softly, "because they aren't frightened by the lights. They *like* them."

Meanwhile, the imps had picked up lanterns and were now skittering away. Allbones's eyes seemed to grow heavy as he watched them go. When he yawned, the roar that came from his throat was so loud it caused the earth to vibrate. Then the manticore stretched out across the courtyard and appeared to fall asleep.

Fifteen minutes passed and the monster didn't stir.

"Let's go," Beatrice whispered.

"We can't reach the door without stepping over him," Teddy said.

"There's a vine growing up the side of the house," Ollie pointed out. "We could climb it to that window."

They emerged from their hiding place into the clearing and looked around uneasily. But nothing moved in the silent heat-shimmering fields.

Beatrice started toward the cottage, with Teddy and Ollie following close behind her. All at once she became aware of a slight breeze on her face. Then she heard a whisper and glanced around at Teddy and Ollie.

"Did either of you say something?" Beatrice asked.

Teddy and Ollie shook their heads. Then Ollie's eyes suddenly opened wide, and he pointed toward the cottage.

Beatrice spun around, expecting to find Allbones awake and coming after them. Then her breath caught in her throat. It wasn't the manticore that Ollie had seen—but the small forest of dead trees that stood around the cottage. It was the trees that were whispering. And they were moving!

Beatrice blinked rapidly several times, so astonished that she thought her imagination must be playing tricks on her. But there they were. At least twenty trees—leafless and bleached like driftwood by the sun—were coming from both sides of the cottage to form a tight cluster. Then—as every nerve in Beatrice's body quivered in shocked disbelief—the trees started *walking* with menacing intent toward the trio.

Beatrice had the crazy thought that they looked like an army of skeletons, glistening white in the burning sun, their skinny arms hanging loosely by their sides as they marched forward. It even seemed that the knotholes and bumps on their trunks had arranged themselves into patterns resembling facial features—the mouths scowling and the eyes radiating evil.

"Enchanted trees," Ollie muttered. "This isn't good."

"Well, don't just stand there!" Teddy exclaimed hysterically.

All three started to run. They raced around the rocks where they had been hiding, and then stopped. There was no place to conceal themselves!

Beatrice glanced back at the trees. They were quickly gaining ground.

"Should we try to make it back to Longshank?" Teddy asked, her breath coming in shallow pants.

"No time," Beatrice said.

"I'd rather run than wait for them to crush us," Ollie said.

But they all knew that running wouldn't save them.

"I'll try something," Beatrice said, hesitating to compose her thoughts. Then she began to chant:

> *Circle of magic, hear my plea,*
> *Send lightning down to every tree*
> *That stalks toward my friends and me.*
> *As my will, so mote it be!*

Instantly, they heard a rumble of thunder. Beatrice looked up and saw black clouds forming overhead. A jagged spear of lightning shot down from the clouds, followed in quick succession by dozens more.

Suddenly there was a loud explosion as lightning struck one of the trees. A horrible scream rose from within its branches and the tree burst into flames. Glowing like a giant torch, it went running off across the barren fields. Soon another tree was struck, then another. Before long, all the trees had fled.

Thoroughly shaken, Beatrice, Teddy, and Ollie sat down to recover. But Beatrice was worried about Allbones. She knew that when he woke up to all that racket and saw burning trees everywhere, he would leave the courtyard to investigate.

Beatrice stood up and peered over the rocks. Sure enough, the manticore was standing outside the gate, his expression fierce as his red eyes moved over the landscape. He would know that some intruder had alerted the trees to danger, and then set them on fire.

"Allbones is on guard," Beatrice whispered. "We may never have a chance to reach Innes."

Ollie crawled over to the rocks and had a look. "He can't stay there forever," Ollie said softly. "We'll just wait."

They took turns watching the cottage. Several hours went by. Beatrice was hungry and thirsty and miserably hot. She was imagining a tall glass of Aunt Primrose's iced moonbeam tea when Teddy suddenly pulled at her arm.

"He's gone inside the courtyard," Teddy said in an excited whisper. "Now he's sitting down."

Beatrice and Teddy bobbed up to look.

The manticore had leaned back against the cottage door. But his rigid posture suggested that he was alert and watchful.

Another hour passed before Allbones began to relax. Finally, he stretched out in front of the door and lay still.

"It might be a trick," Ollie said. "Let's give him a while."

After forty-five minutes, Teddy whispered, "I can hear him snoring, and I can't take any more waiting. I'm ready to go!"

Beatrice glanced at Ollie. He nodded.

"Okay," Beatrice said. "If we come in from the left, he won't be able to see us approach the cottage, even if he is awake. Just be quiet."

"Dally Rumpe may have set up other traps," Ollie said. "Enchanted windows or something."

Beatrice shrugged. "Well, we won't know till we try it."

They made their way quickly across the clearing to the side of the house. Beatrice listened for Allbones's approach. Hearing nothing, she gave Teddy and Ollie a thumbs-up sign.

They threw back their heads and peered up at the window.

"It's higher than it looked from out there," Ollie said softly. Then he grinned, gamely took hold of the vine, and started to climb.

Beatrice came next, then Teddy. As she inched her way up the twisted stalk, Beatrice kept her ears attuned to any sound that might mean someone was coming. But all she heard was the rustling of dry leaves as they climbed the vine.

They were so small, it took a while to reach the

window ledge. And then they faced another problem. The window was open, but it was covered by screen wire.

Ollie peered into the room to make certain that no one was there. Then he dug into the pocket of his jeans and produced a tiny pocketknife. He began to saw away at the screen one wire at a time. Meanwhile, Beatrice and Teddy looked inside. The room was furnished like a sunporch, with wicker chairs and a small settee. A ceiling fan turned lazily overhead. They could hear the faint sound of music coming from somewhere within the house.

A few minutes later, Ollie said, "That should do it."

He crawled through the hole in the screen, followed by Beatrice and Teddy.

Once inside, they leaped off the window ledge into the soft cushion of a chair. It was like bouncing on a trampoline. They held onto the skirt of the chair and rappelled down its side to the floor.

Beatrice led the way across the room. When she reached the door, she peered cautiously around the door frame into a dimly lit corridor.

And there—leaning against the wall with his arms casually crossed—was Allbones.

He grinned fiercely at their stunned faces and said in his strange musical voice, "It's so nice to finally meet you. Won't you join me for a cup of tea?"

17

Dally Rumpe

Beatrice stared at the manticore. Up close he was even more terrible than she had first thought. His lips were like glistening gray slugs, parted now in a hideous grin that revealed all too clearly those yellowed daggerlike fangs. And his eyes! The irises were a clouded milky white, gleaming eerily against his red eyeballs.

"Cat got your tongue?" Allbones asked slyly. "You seem surprised to find me here. Did you really think I couldn't sense the presence of *witches* when you were spying on me?" He said the word *witches* as if it left a nasty taste in his mouth.

Beatrice was quickly recovering from her shock, and now she was scared. She fought back the impulse to run, realizing that any movement might result in the manticore lashing out with one of his great paws and squashing her like a bug. She glanced at Teddy and Ollie and saw the same barely controlled panic in their faces.

"I know all about your expedition to Winter Wood," Allbones went on conversationally. "I can't imagine how any self-respecting dragon could allow himself to be bamboozled by a bunch of foolish children. I just hope you're not counting on that happening again," he added, his lips spreading into a wider grin, "or on leaving Werewolf Close alive."

Beatrice inhaled deeply and blew her bangs out of her eyes. *Keep him talking,* she thought. *Maybe we'll find some way out of this.*

Then she said the first thing that popped into her mind. "Are you Dally Rumpe?"

The manticore feigned surprise, but he was obviously pleased by the question. "My goodness, no! You've already *met* the master. I am simply Dally Rumpe's devoted servant, with orders to end your bothersome meddling once and for all."

Ollie moved forward to stand beside Beatrice. "Is Dally Rumpe here?" he asked. Beatrice thought he sounded calm and brave.

"Why, yes," Allbones said. "Would you like one last meeting with the master? I'm sure he would be delighted."

Beatrice couldn't think of anything she wanted less, but it would buy them time. "Of course we want to see Dally Rumpe," she replied.

Beatrice noticed that Teddy appeared pale and shaken, as if the last of her courage had trickled away. That's when Beatrice remembered that they had one weapon left. The amulets! Yorick had said if they could face the manticore with true fearlessness, the monster's power over them would dissolve. Could the stones give them the courage they needed?

"Well, come along then," Allbones said. "I've wasted enough time with you today. Walk to the end of this hall and through that door. I'll be right behind you, so don't even think about trying to get away."

"Will Innes be there?" Beatrice asked.

"Innes is *always* here," Allbones replied.

As they started down the hall, Beatrice slipped her hand into the pocket of her jeans. She closed her fingers around the amulet and brought her clenched fist slowly to her chest.

Beatrice glanced at Teddy and Ollie, who were walking on either side of her, and opened her hand discreetly. When Teddy and Ollie saw the stone in Beatrice's palm, comprehension dawned in their faces.

"Don't let him see," Beatrice whispered.

As they continued toward the door at the end of the hall, Beatrice cut her eyes from Teddy to Ollie and back again. She saw them reaching for their own amulets.

"At the count of three," Beatrice said under her breath, "face him. Think *courage*."

Beatrice took a few steps, then whispered, "One, two, three."

They turned around together, holding their amulets tightly. The manticore towered over them, his glittering eyes and enormous fangs just as terrible as ever. But Beatrice realized suddenly that she was no longer afraid.

The stone works! she thought, her astonishment and joy spilling over into laughter. Then Teddy and Ollie were laughing, too.

"We aren't afraid of you," Beatrice said boldly to the manticore. "You have no power over us."

Allbones looked confused, then his face contorted

with anger. He took a step toward them, but Beatrice, Teddy, and Ollie stood their ground. They held their amulets up toward him.

Allbones faltered, standing perfectly still and looking at the three tiny figures at his feet with a perplexed expression. Then his eyes narrowed and he said quietly, "You'd do well to be afraid."

The manticore took another step.

"Stop right there," Ollie said, his voice so forceful that Beatrice flinched. "You can't harm us."

Beatrice's eyes darted back to Allbones. "We aren't afraid of you," she repeated.

"We aren't afraid," Teddy and Ollie said together. "We aren't afraid, we aren't afraid, we aren't afraid . . ."

As the chanting went on, Allbones grabbed at his chest. He staggered back, staring at them in bewilderment and horror. And then it happened. The manticore disappeared. Just like that, he was gone!

Beatrice, Teddy, and Ollie stood frozen for a moment, their eyes fixed on the spot where Allbones had been only seconds before.

"Could he come back?" Teddy asked softly.

"I don't know," Beatrice said.

Seconds ticked by and the manticore didn't reappear. Beatrice began to feel her muscles relax a little. She turned to her friends and saw that they had silly grins on their faces.

Then they heard the voice behind them.

"Well done," the unknown speaker said heartily. "I never imagined that you were capable of facing the manticore without fear."

Beatrice's knees went weak and the room began to spin. Sheer will kept her standing.

"Now turn around," the voice coaxed them. "You were on your way to meet me, I believe? I've been waiting for this moment, Beatrice Bailiwick. Ever since our last encounter."

18

Facing the Music

Beatrice recognized that voice. She knew Dally Rumpe's identity even before she turned to look. Beatrice supposed that she should have been shocked. But somehow, she wasn't.

She turned almost mechanically to face Dally Rumpe. Tilting her head back, Beatrice's eyes traveled slowly up the blue cotton robes—and came to rest on the pretty face of Molly Wilder.

Beatrice's gaze shifted from the little-girl ponytails to the wide smile—which, incredibly, still seemed genuinely open and innocent. Then Beatrice noticed the flute in the sorcerer's hand and remembered the music they had heard from outside.

The smile faded from Molly's lips. She studied Beatrice with eyes that had suddenly become shrewd. "You don't look especially surprised," she said, sounding displeased.

"I'm not," Beatrice admitted. "The night of the picnic, after you played the flute so beautifully and Aunt Primrose praised you for your talents, I wondered why you stayed in a little place like Friar's Lantern. Working for Aunt

Primrose and running after Bing didn't seem like much of a life. I thought something was wrong."

"What's wrong is Primrose Merriwether lording it over everyone," Molly snapped. "She puts on a good act, making people believe she's *so* kind and *so* giving—opening her home and her heart to charity cases like Bing and me. But you know why she does it, don't you? So she can have someone to order around and feel superior to."

"She gave you a job," Beatrice said, meanwhile glancing over the sorcerer's shoulder in hopes of seeing Innes, "and a place to live."

"She gave me *servitude!*" Molly spat out the words contemptuously. "Primrose Merriwether is such a phony. Unlike her sister," the sorcerer added with a hint of amusement. "Laurel is vain and selfish—and refreshingly honest. She never did like me, and didn't pretend to." Then Molly's face hardened again. "Do-gooders like Primrose make me sick!"

A young woman had come to stand in the doorway behind Molly. She was tall and fair, with emerald green eyes and a thick braid of light brown hair falling over the shoulder of her pale green robes. Beatrice realized that she was finally in the presence of Innes of Bailiwick. Then Beatrice noticed that Innes was also holding a flute, and seeing the two of them together, she had the ridiculous thought that Molly and Innes could have been friends under different circumstances. Just two young girls sharing confidences and a love of music.

Innes's expression was neutral, showing neither fear of her jailer nor surprise at the unexpected arrival of three small bedraggled creatures who seemed to have stepped willingly into Dally Rumpe's lair. *She must have no idea,* Beatrice thought, *that we came here to help her.* Then Beatrice's heart sank at the absurdity of that. She was in no position to help anyone, not even herself.

"So nothing you told us was true," Beatrice said weakly to Molly, playing for time. "The death of your parents, attending the witch academy in Friar's Lantern—"

"It was *all* true," the sorcerer said, grinning. "Only none of it happened to *me*. The real Molly Wilder lived in Friar's Lantern and went to the academy until she was twelve. Her family moved away, and a few months later, they were all killed in a boating accident. But no one in Friar's Lantern knew that."

"How did *you* know?" Beatrice demanded.

Molly frowned at Beatrice's tone, but eager to flaunt her cleverness, she replied, "I knew you would be coming to Werewolf Close next. Isn't that what it says in *The Bailiwick Family History?*" she asked, mocking Beatrice. "And I needed an identity, fast. Birth and death records are cross-referenced, so I looked for someone who had been born in Friar's Lantern and died elsewhere. After I came up with Molly's name, I contacted a young witch who had just arrived in the village to serve in the Witches' Service Corps—"

Teddy's hand flew to her mouth. "Fillian Hawthorn," she murmured.

"That's right," Molly said impatiently. "I claimed to be a manager at the Witches' Institute, in the Hall of Witch Records. I told him an employee of mine had made a terrible mistake—declaring a whole family dead when we didn't think that was the case—and I was trying to save

195

the witch's job. Hawthorne agreed to ask around—discreetly, of course—to see if anyone in Friar's Lantern knew for certain whether they were alive." Molly smirked. "He came back saying that everyone assumed they were still alive, but no one had heard from them since they moved. Of course, when I showed up on Primrose's doorstep—the grieving orphan—I had to break the sad news to her about my parents' untimely demise."

"Then Fillian didn't know your real identity," Teddy said.

Molly shot her a look of annoyance. "I'm *very* good at hiding whatever I need to hide. And the fact that Hawthorne has his eye on high places helped. He was thrilled to have someone at the Institute in his debt—and he didn't question anything I told him after I suggested that he come for lunch sometime and meet my good friend Thaddeus Thigpin."

"But how did you know what Molly Wilder looked like?" Beatrice asked.

"The library has witch academy yearbooks for the past fifty years," the sorcerer said smugly. "I even copied the hairstyle from her class photo."

"Didn't people ask you questions about your—I mean, *Molly's* parents?" Beatrice persisted, still watching Innes out of the corner of her eye. "Weren't you afraid of saying something that would give you away?"

"They were all too *good* and *kind* to bring up the painful subject of my poor deceased mother and father," Molly said with disdain. "And who actually *talked* to me, anyway? Primrose was too busy bossing me around to ask any questions, and I never had time to exchange more than a 'merry meet' and a 'merry part' with anyone else. And speaking of questions," she said, her tone suddenly sharp, "I think you've asked enough."

Molly turned abruptly to Innes. "We have guests, my dear," she said, with an ironic emphasis on the word *guests*. "Unfortunately, they won't be with us very long. Shall we entertain them before they have to leave?"

Innes didn't reply but dutifully lifted the flute to her lips.

Molly looked back at Beatrice. "Primrose was right about one thing," she said. "I *am* a brilliant musician. Witch Innes, on the other hand, is merely passable. I hope you'll overlook her inadequacies."

Molly positioned her flute and the two began to play. Beatrice was vaguely aware that the music was beautiful, and that Innes's part sounded far better than passable. But uppermost in her mind were thoughts of survival.

She stood quietly for a few moments, until Molly seemed totally engrossed in the music. Then Beatrice began to chant under her breath:

> By the power of the south,
> By the beauty of the light,
> Release this circle, I do implore,
> Make all that's wrong revert to right.

Teddy and Ollie edged closer to Beatrice, as if to give her support.

Beatrice glanced up at Molly and saw that she was playing with her eyes closed, apparently oblivious to everything around her.

Beatrice continued to chant:

> By the power of the south,
> By the spirit of the wood,
> Release this circle, I do implore,
> Make all that's evil revert to good.

The music leaped, then fell, like a delicate bird soaring overhead.

> By the power of the south,
> By the chant of witch's song,
> Release this circle, I do implore,
> Make all that's weak revert to strong.

All at once, the music stopped. Beatrice's eyes darted upward and she saw Molly staring down at her with a condescending smile.

"Do you really think," the sorcerer said, "that I'm stupid enough to let you finish the spell while I graciously serenade you? *You* are the stupid one, Beatrice Bailiwick."

Molly's expression suddenly turned ugly. At that moment, the rounded prettiness of the sorcerer's face began to change before Beatrice's startled eyes. Flesh once pink and youthful turned coarse and sallow. The face became grotesquely haggard, with sunken cheeks and deep bony eye sockets. The dark eyes that held Beatrice entranced were no longer those of an innocent young girl, but of a demonic beast.

In a sickening instant, Beatrice realized that she was catching a glimpse of the real Dally Rumpe—and what she saw when she looked into those cold inhuman eyes made her skin crawl.

"There's a hungry manticore waiting for you outside," the sorcerer said in a voice that was chillingly matter-of-fact. "He prefers his meals in the open air."

Dally Rumpe kicked at Beatrice and her friends to make them move. The three stumbled along to the end of the hallway, where Innes stood aside to let them pass. Beatrice heard a whispered, "I'm sorry," as she brushed against the hem of Innes's robes.

Beatrice's mind was working furiously as she stepped out the front door into the stifling heat of the courtyard. Then she saw Allbones standing beside a cauldron. He was adding wood to a fire that already blazed beneath the huge black kettle.

The manticore watched Beatrice and her friends intently as they approached. One look at his bared fangs and Beatrice could see that he was furious.

"You're worthless!" Dally Rumpe shouted at the manticore, raising a threatening hand as if to strike the beast. The fingers were now long and gnarled, with sharp hooked claws. "Do you think you can handle it from here without messing up?"

Allbones lowered his head in a submissive gesture and replied softly, "I will do your bidding, Master."

But there was nothing docile in the manticore's outraged eyes as they shifted back to Beatrice and her friends. He had been humiliated and was determined to have his revenge.

His face shimmering in the steam that rose from the bubbling cauldron, Allbones took a step toward them.

Beatrice cringed, knowing what their fates would be. The monster meant to boil them alive!

As the manticore moved closer, Beatrice felt a wave of dizziness wash over her. She took a deep breath to steady herself and looked around in desperation. Teddy and Ollie were staring in horror at the boiling pot, and Beatrice knew that they understood Dally Rumpe's plans for them. The evil sorcerer—who now bore only a feeble resemblance to young Molly Wilder—was gazing in demented bliss into the fire.

Beatrice considered grabbing for Teddy and Ollie's hands and making a futile run for it. But before the thought was fully formed, something came flying through the air and landed on Allbones's head. The manticore let out a startled roar.

Beatrice peered at the greenish blob between Allbones's horns and saw that it was Longshank! The little water leaper was gripping the manticore's mane while Allbones tried to shake him loose.

The manticore began to swat at his head with his enormous paws. But clever Longshank shinnied up one of the monster's razor-sharp horns, and Allbones pierced his own paw pad when he grabbed for the water leaper.

Dally Rumpe was beside himself with fury. He paced back and forth across the courtyard, shrieking at the manticore, "You fool! Is a frog going to outsmart you now? It's over, Allbones! I'll take care of you *and* these witches!"

Suddenly the sorcerer's eyes fell on Beatrice. He spun around and came hurtling toward her. Instinctively, Beatrice ran. But in no time, Dally Rumpe's massive shadow had engulfed her. Beatrice felt the sorcerer's breath like a wind gust as one of his sharp claws nicked her arm. She screamed, and in a burst of speed, darted into a clump of bushes.

Drawn by the sight of Innes watching from the doorway, Beatrice started running through the undergrowth toward the house. Glancing over her shoulder, she was amazed to see that Dally Rumpe hadn't followed her. Instead, he had gone after Teddy and Ollie—and was clutching them in his tightly clenched fists. They were kicking furiously to free themselves. Ignoring them, Dally Rumpe came striding across the courtyard toward Beatrice.

Gasping for breath, Beatrice stumbled toward Innes. "Stay right there," she said, panting, and began to chant:

> By the power of the south,
> By the goodness of the dove,
> Release this circle, I do implore,
> Make all that's hateful revert to love.
>
> Heed this charm, attend to me,
> As my word, so mote it be!

Only steps away from her now, Dally Rumpe realized what Beatrice had done. He looked at her in shocked disbelief. "It's impossible!" the sorcerer screeched. "You can't have done it again."

But Beatrice could already feel a cool breeze on her face. Leaves were bursting forth on long-dead trees, grass was sprouting underfoot, and the sun overhead was changing from angry orange to gentle gold.

The manticore had vanished, and now Dally Rumpe fell limply to the ground. Teddy and Ollie scrambled from the loosening grip of his claws and started running toward Beatrice.

Writhing in pain, the sorcerer shrieked his rage and frustration. Eyes as empty as darkened windows clung to Beatrice's face—seeming intent on memorizing every curve and plane—until they rolled back into Dally Rumpe's head. The sorcerer's body began to blur, then evaporate into a cloud of mist.

As a breeze swept through and carried the mist away, Beatrice heard Dally Rumpe's voice one last time. In a hoarse whisper that made the hair stand up on the back of her neck, the sorcerer vowed, "Next time, Beatrice Bailiwick, I won't wait for you to come to me."

19

ℋomecoming

Beatrice looked around for Teddy and Ollie. They were standing nearby, gazing in wonder at their new surroundings. The parched earth had been transformed and was now covered in a lush carpet of green. The once harsh light was shimmering gold, as if sunbeams had been ground into a fine dust and then flung into the air. The breeze was gentle and pleasant. And most incredibly of all, Beatrice could look out over the trees and see a clear blue sky. The enchanted fog had disappeared.

Beatrice spotted Longshank sitting in the grass with a satisfied look on his face—a face that Beatrice would never again think of as ugly. Cayenne was lying a short distance away, holding her leash firmly with her front paws as she tried to wrestle her way out of the detested harness.

Beatrice waded through the thick cool grass to stand with them.

"Dally Rumpe had us," Beatrice said to Longshank. "If you hadn't come when you did—"

"I don't even want to think about it!" Longshank's voice rose sharply in distress. "I waited through that terrible storm, and then I heard all the screaming—and saw trees burning . . ." His eyes were opened wide in his broad little face. "But you told me to stay put, so I did. Until finally, I couldn't stand not knowing what was happening, so Cayenne and I came to look for you. But you weren't here, so we waited. A *long time*. Then you came out from the house, and that monster was there . . ." The water leaper began to tremble. "I was scared," he said, looking down in shame at his webbed toes. "Really scared."

"But in spite of that, you came to save us," Beatrice said gently. "We're in your debt, Longshank."

The water leaper glanced up shyly and grinned.

Teddy and Ollie had come to join them. They were all watching Innes now. She was coming slowly down the steps and looking around in astonishment. Then Innes saw Beatrice and her friends. A radiant smile broke out across her face as she started toward them.

Longshank leaped to his feet when Innes drew near and bent low in a courtly bow. "My lady, good witch Innes," he murmured.

Innes laughed, delighted and obviously still a little dazed. "Thank you—*all* of you—for what you've done," she said in a rush. "And forgive me for having to ask—but who *are* you? And how did you come to be here?"

"I'm Beatrice Bailiwick—"

"Oh, my!" Innes's hands flew to her face and she stared in amazement at Beatrice. "You're a Bailiwick witch! After all this time—and all the witches who have failed—"

"And these are my friends," Beatrice said, and introduced everyone to Innes.

Innes crouched down so that she could see them all

better. "What about my father and sisters?" she asked anxiously. "Are they still held captive by Dally Rumpe?"

"Your sister Rhona was freed two months ago," Beatrice said.

Innes drew in a quick breath and her face lit up at the news.

"Dally Rumpe can never set foot in that region again, just as he can never return to Werewolf Close." Beatrice hesitated, wishing she didn't have to tell Innes the next part, and then she said gently, "Bromwich and your other two sisters are still Dally Rumpe's prisoners."

Innes's happiness dimmed, but then a hopeful look crept into her eyes. "Can I assume that you'll be going to help them, as well?" she asked.

Beatrice felt a knot forming in her stomach. She still couldn't quite believe that they had survived the werewolves and the fog, not to mention Allbones and Dally Rumpe. And now they would have to do it all over again. For a moment, she wished that she could do as Aunt Primrose wanted—just walk away from these Bailiwick witches, and maybe even settle down to a fun and interesting life in Friar's Lantern. Then Beatrice felt a flood of guilt. Her life was in the mortal world with her mother and father. She couldn't stay in the Sphere when her mother wasn't even allowed to visit her here! And as for turning her back on Bromwich and his daughters . . .

Beatrice sighed. "We're going to try to help them," she said.

Innes's face relaxed and she reached out to touch Beatrice's arm with the tips of her fingers. "I can never thank you enough," she said softly.

"You know, Innes," Teddy said, "you and Rhona can see each other now. I imagine she's already heard through the witches' grapevine that you're free. It wouldn't surprise me if she showed up here very soon."

"I can hardly believe it," Innes murmured, her green eyes shining. "I'll actually be seeing my sister again—after two hundred years."

About that time, they all noticed that people had emerged from their cabins and were looking at their changed surroundings in stunned disbelief. Innes smiled, watching them.

"It's been so hard for them," she said quietly. "It will probably take a while for them to adjust to—*being happy*," she finished, beaming at Beatrice and her friends.

"There's something I have to ask you," Beatrice said suddenly. "People in Friar's Lantern believe you have a fortune in gold hidden away. Is that true?"

Innes's eyes twinkled. "There isn't any gold," she said. "Shall I tell you how that myth started? It was right after Dally Rumpe cast his spell," Innes said, her face growing somber as she remembered, "and I was in shock. I didn't know then what had happened to my father and sisters, and I was very frightened. But I thought maybe there was a way to escape. I had a few gold coins in the pocket of my cloak, and I tried bribing the manticore to release me."

Shaking her head, Innes said wryly, "Naive of me, wasn't it, to think that one of Dally Rumpe's monsters might actually let me go? Of course, Allbones told Dally Rumpe, who became convinced that I had a treasure concealed somewhere in the Close. He came to me day after day, demanding to know where it was. I told him truthfully that there was no gold, but he didn't believe me. He had these horrible little creatures—" Innes shivered at the thought of them, "—tear the house apart. Of course, they found nothing. Finally, Dally Rumpe stopped mentioning the gold."

"That's probably because he thought it had already been stolen," Ollie said. "For years, witches in Friar's Lantern have told stories about people somehow making it into Werewolf Close and stealing the gold and then burying it in the swamps around the village."

"And when we first saw Allbones, he was sending out a troop of hideous little hobgoblins or something—the same creatures who searched your house, most likely—" Teddy said, "to hunt for gold in the swamps."

Innes laughed in delight. "I'm so glad to hear that Dally Rumpe has been searching all these years for a treasure that doesn't exist."

"But that means the people in Friar's Lantern will lose something they've come to love," Beatrice said. "They all talk about mysterious lights that move through the swamps at night—the village was even named after them!—and all the time, it was the lanterns carried by Dally Rumpe's creatures as they searched for your gold. It may sound silly," Beatrice added, "but the witches in Friar's Lantern are very fond of their lights—I don't think they want the mystery to be solved."

"It isn't silly at all," Innes replied. "Witches need their magic and mystery."

"But now the lights won't be there," Beatrice said, feeling unaccountably sad. *Maybe I need that magic and mystery myself*, she thought.

"They could be," Innes said quickly, her face becoming animated. "I can send people out with lights—say, three or four times a week. Would that be often enough? They can roam through the swamps around the village carrying their lanterns."

Beatrice grinned. "You'd do that?" she asked.

"Of course," Innes said. "They're our neighbors, and I want to help them. But I'll need time to ask for volunteers. What if we start next week?"

Beatrice was smiling broadly at Innes. "That would be great," she said.

It was time for Innes to go introduce herself to the people of Werewolf Close. She asked Beatrice and her friends to join her so that everyone could thank them properly. But Beatrice remembered all too well the overwhelming displays of gratitude and affection in Winter Wood and wanted to avoid having to make another speech.

"Our friends are waiting for us," Beatrice said. "We should be going."

Innes nodded. "I understand. But promise me, Beatrice, that I'll see you again someday."

"Of course."

"When the last region of Bailiwick has been freed, and the kingdom has been reunited," Innes said softly, "all of you must join us at my father's castle. We'll have a feast in your honor."

"We wouldn't miss it!" Teddy declared, no doubt already imagining what it would be like to attend a banquet in a real Traditional witch castle in the Witches' Sphere.

It was nearly dark when their boat docked at the Friar's Lantern pier, but still light enough for them to see Peregrine standing on the wharf waiting for them.

"I can't believe you're here!" Beatrice greeted her witch adviser as she clamored out of the boat. Then she grinned. In his dull brown robes, with his ears sticking out from his toast-colored hair and his mouth stretched into a crooked little smile, he was a sight for sore eyes. Before she realized what she was doing, Beatrice bent down and gave him a big hug. Peregrine's ears turned crimson and he ducked his head.

"I've been sent as your official escort," Peregrine said, looking at her through lowered lashes.

"Why do I need an escort?" Beatrice asked as the others got out of the boat and gathered around them.

"Well—you see—" Peregrine cleared his throat nervously. "Actually, that's a secret. So I can't tell you."

Beatrice glanced at Teddy, Ollie, Cyrus, and Longshank, who were all brimming over with good cheer.

"We wouldn't want you to tell a secret when you aren't supposed to," Ollie said.

"But we're dying of curiosity," Teddy added. "So lead on, Peregrine!"

Beatrice picked up Cayenne, who was now blissfully free of harness and leash, and looked around for Xan. She was surprised to see him climbing back into the boat.

"Aren't you coming with us?" Beatrice asked him.

"Aunt Primrose will want to thank you—actually, she'll want to smother you with kisses—and Aunt Laurel," Beatrice added with a twinkle, "has some crow to eat. And you wouldn't want to miss that."

Peregrine had come over to the edge of the pier and was looking down at Xan. "Yes, you have to come," the witch adviser said firmly. "This is for you, too."

"*What* is for him?" Beatrice asked.

Realizing that he had said too much, Peregrine started turning red again. "*All right*," he said, "they're giving you a party. As soon as word of your success reached Friar's Lantern, everyone in the village started making the arrangements. It's in your honor," he said to Beatrice. "And Teddy's and Ollie's and Cyrus's and Cayenne's and Longshank's." Then his eyes shifted toward the boat. "And Xan's."

"See there!" Beatrice said to Xan. "You can't leave."

Xan hadn't moved from the boat. He was scowling —but just barely. "Uh—I'm not good at parties," he mumbled.

"But this one is in your honor," Beatrice persisted. "They know now that they've been wrong about you. Won't you give them a chance to make it up to you?"

Xan's scowl deepened. He glanced up at her and grumbled, "You've been a lot of trouble ever since I met you."

"But she grows on you," Ollie said cheerfully.

"Okay, I'll come," Xan said gruffly, "but I have to take care of something first."

Beatrice looked at him doubtfully. "You're just saying that. You won't really come."

"Yes, I will." He sounded a little less grumpy. "Save me some food."

After the boat left, the rest of them set off with Peregrine up Will-o'-the-wisp Road. Beatrice was feeling relieved and happy—and just a bit let down because she was sure Xan had no intention of coming to the party. And she really would have liked to see him become an accepted member of the community. It would kind of tie things up for her. But Xan had to make his own decisions.

Beatrice had assumed that they would be going back to Merriwether House, but Peregrine led them into Cattail Court. Everyone in the village must have been there, and when they saw Beatrice and her friends, they started to applaud and cheer.

"Oh, I wish I had my red hat," Teddy said. But hat or no hat, she looked ecstatic.

Beatrice noticed that Ollie and Cyrus were grinning, a little embarrassed, maybe, as people they didn't even know rushed forward to shake their hands, but basically delighted. Beatrice was pleased, as well—Who wouldn't be?—but she couldn't shake that old feeling that she didn't deserve all this attention. By the time she had made it through the crowd of enthusiastic admirers to The Cat and the Fiddle, she was wishing that she had fled with Xan.

But then Primrose and Laurel were hugging her, with both aunts tearing up a little, and Beatrice was being swept inside. The restaurant was so packed with people, there was barely room to walk.

Beatrice and her friends were led to a long table where several guests were already seated. Yorick Figlock was there, with Old Foxy fast asleep on his shoulder and Bing sitting beside him.

Bing grinned at Beatrice. "Well, we did it, didn't we?"

Beatrice nodded, thinking that maybe there was hope for Primrose's lost sheep after all. "But we never would have gotten across the river if you hadn't outsmarted the Shellycoats," she said.

"That's just what I told Miss Primrose," Bing replied.

When Beatrice and her friends had sat down, Yorick stood and raised his glass of witches' brew.

"A toast to my new young friends," Yorick said, gazing mistily at Beatrice, "who know the true meaning of courage."

Beatrice suddenly remembered the amulet and reached into her pocket. She held it up, grinning at Yorick. "It worked," she said. "Your amulets gave us courage."

Yorick's face rearranged itself into a grin that was decidedly wicked. "Those *amulets*," he said, his pale eyes twinkling, "are nothing more than pretty stones I picked up along the river."

Beatrice blinked.

"You mean they weren't even magical?" Teddy demanded.

Yorick shook his head. "You had the courage inside you all along. The stones just gave you the confidence to find it."

"Will you be seeing your family soon?" Ollie asked the old witch.

Yorick nodded happily. "As soon as this party's over, Old Foxy and I will be heading for Werewolf Close. I think we'll probably end up staying."

Laurel came bustling over carrying four blue-gray boxes.

"Our hats!" Teddy exclaimed.

"I knew you'd want to wear them tonight," a beaming Laurel said.

"Right," Cyrus said wearily.

They put on their Laurel Merriwether originals to the *oohs* and *ahhs* of the excited designer. Beatrice found herself feeling almost like a Traditional witch with the blue velvet hat on her head.

Then Puddifoot and Glee started bringing in trays of food. Beatrice was a little surprised when a sandwich was placed in front of her. With all the hoopla, she had kind of expected Aunt Primrose to go all out.

"It's serpent's egg salad," Cyrus said under his breath. "I *can't stand* serpents eggs!"

Primrose sat down in the chair across from Beatrice. "I know it's not very *festive*," Primrose said with a worried look, "but Laurel and I never learned to cook, and this is about all I know how to make."

Beatrice grinned, thinking of her mother. The cooking gene must have skipped the Merriwethers altogether.

"And you know," Primrose went on with a sigh, "I don't have a chef anymore. Can you believe it?" she demanded. "Dally Rumpe was in my very own kitchen chopping lizard gizzards!"

About that time, Fillian Hawthorne walked up to the table.

"Congratulations, Beatrice," he said, looking stiff and uncomfortable. "I never thought you could do it, but apparently, you've proven me wrong. I'm very happy for you."

"I imagine you'd be happier," Ollie said drily, "if you had broken the spell yourself."

"That goes without saying," Fillian replied without a trace of embarrassment. "It could have added a big punch to my résumé. I specifically asked for an assignment in Friar's Lantern, thinking I'd work on it while I was here." He glanced from Ollie to Beatrice, obviously annoyed. "But you four beat me to it."

"Eight, actually," Beatrice said brightly. "Counting Cayenne, Longshank, Xan, and Bing."

Fillian's face darkened. Beatrice assumed it was the mention of Xan's name that got to him most.

"My congratulations to you all," Fillian muttered, and left quickly.

"Beatrice," Ollie said, leaning close so the others couldn't hear. "I have a confession to make."

Beatrice noted his serious expression, and said, "What is it?"

Ollie's face turned pink as he glared down at his plate. "It's just that—Teddy was right," he burst out. "From the moment we met him, Fillian seemed like such a show-off—and I guess I *was* a little jealous." He looked up at Beatrice and his face turned pinker. "The worst part was, you seemed to be impressed by him."

A slow smile spread across Beatrice's lips. She hadn't expected this, but she didn't mind at all. "I *was* impressed at first," she admitted. "Then I began to realize that Fillian is really shallow. It's the people I've known the longest—the people I trust and care about—who impress me the most."

Now Beatrice was blushing and looking down at the table, and Ollie was grinning from ear to ear.

Just then, Peregrine skittered over to Beatrice. "The

Witches' Executive Committee has just arrived," he said, sounding breathless and a little anxious.

That's when Beatrice remembered that they had gone to Werewolf Close without the committee's knowledge or approval. Suddenly she had a sick feeling in the pit of her stomach. No matter what she had told Teddy, Beatrice didn't believe Dr. Thigpin was here to congratulate them for going off on their own.

Beatrice turned around and saw the committee coming through the door. Thirteen witches—with Thaddeus Thigpin in the lead.

20

A Witch of Friar's Lantern

The crowd parted and conversation stopped abruptly as the Witches' Executive Committee swept into the room. Everyone at Beatrice's table got nervously to their feet.

"This is the first time in fifty years that they've made a public appearance in Friar's Lantern," Primrose whispered to Beatrice.

Beatrice took a deep breath and blew her bangs out of her eyes—just as Thaddeus Thigpin stepped up to the table.

He was scowling, of course, but Beatrice couldn't tell if it was a deeper scowl than usual. She glanced over the director's shoulder and caught sight of Dr. Meadowmouse, who appeared pleasantly serene, and then Dr. Featherstone, who was positively beaming. *Okay,* Beatrice thought, *I can't be in that much trouble.*

But then Dr. Thigpin began to speak—to bark, actually—his pale blue eyes cutting through her like a sharp sliver of ice.

"*Never*—in the many years that I have served as director of the Witches' Institute—have I known a *witch*—young or *old*—Traditional or *Reform*—to act with such *glaring* irresponsibility—with such *foolhardiness*—with such disregard for the *rules* upon which this governing body is based—"

Dr. Thigpin paused to catch his breath, but his icy stare never wavered from Beatrice's face.

"Whatever your eventual classification," he went on, "you are a maverick witch, Ms. Bailiwick!" His nostrils were flaring now, and his bushy white eyebrows quivered with every word. "And, let me tell you, I don't approve of maverick witches!"

At that moment, Dr. Featherstone stepped forward and touched his arm. Dr. Thigpin shook her hand off, still glaring at Beatrice.

"Thaddeus," Aura Featherstone said softly, "there's no rule that says they had to wait for our instructions. Remember what the Legal Department told you."

"But there *is* such a thing as respect for proper channels," Dr. Thigpin thundered. "There *are* such things as tradition and protocol—"

"And there are such things as initiative and courage," Dr. Featherstone said lightly. "Would you like Leopold and me to continue with this while you get yourself something to drink?"

Dr. Thigpin seemed torn between the responsibilities of his position and much-needed refreshments. The refreshments won.

"Thank you, Aura," Dr. Thigpin said stiffly.

Then he and the rest of the committee, with the

exception of Drs. Featherstone and Meadowmouse, made a beeline for Puddifoot, who was bringing in a tray of drinks.

Aura Featherstone seemed to visibly relax once the director was gone. She looked at Beatrice, her eyes sparkling, and said, "First, we want to tell you how proud we are of all of you." Dr. Featherstone glanced around the table to include Beatrice's friends, her gaze lingering on Longshank. "From what I've been told, that was some leaping you did," she said to the water leaper.

Longshank dropped his eyes shyly.

"And some guiding you did," Dr. Featherstone said to Cayenne, who regarded the witch with a blank owl-eyed stare.

"All of you are to be commended," Dr. Featherstone continued. "As you probably expected, you won't be classified just yet—" Here she glanced at Teddy and was rewarded with a predictable look of irritation, "—but that day is coming, I promise you!"

"Meanwhile," Dr. Meadowmouse said, "you can go back to your lives in the mortal world and get some rest. You've earned it," he said kindly.

"And when the time is right," Dr. Featherstone said to Beatrice, "you'll be contacted about starting the next part of the test. That will take you to the eastern region of Bailiwick."

Sea-Dragon Bay, Beatrice thought, hoping that Dr. Featherstone wouldn't notice her sigh. *Here we go again . . .*

"I understand that Bailiwicks still live in the surrounding area," Dr. Meadowmouse said to Beatrice.

"Perhaps you can get to know some of your father's family."

That gave Beatrice something to think about. She made a mental note: *Ask Dad if he has any secrets he hasn't told me about.*

After Drs. Featherstone and Meadowmouse had wandered off to join the rest of the committee, Teddy said mournfully to Beatrice, "They're never going to classify us. I'll be rocking my grandchildren and you'll call and say, 'Guess what, Teddy! The committee says it's time for our eighty-seventh test.'"

Beatrice grinned. "At least you won't be reading the kiddies some lame fairy tale at bedtime. You can give them nightmares with real-life adventures."

"That's right," Cyrus jumped in. "'Tonight, children, I'm going to tell you a terrifying tale called *Teddy and the Big Red Hat*.'"

"Very funny," Teddy muttered, but she didn't look quite so despondent as she bit into her serpent's egg sandwich.

After dinner, Magnus Pinch brought out a tin whistle and began to play a lively tune. He was stomping his foot in time to the music and actually seemed to be enjoying himself.

"Who would have thought it?" Beatrice said to Ollie. "Do you think he really is smuggling in illegal herbs?"

Ollie shook his head. "No, I just think he's weird."

Soon everyone was singing along with the music.

Being a witch is a very good thing.
We can hoot and holler and dance and sing,

Or fly through the air like a bat on its wing.
Being a witch is a fabulous thing!

Being a cat is nearly as nice.
They break all the rules without thinking twice.
When you're feeling let down, they bring you dead mice.
Being a cat is incredibly nice!

Even Skye Drummond was singing. Beatrice was a little surprised to see Skye there at all. She had just decided to make one more attempt at conversation with her mother's former friend when she noticed the front door opening. And then Xan walked in! He stopped just inside the doorway, as if uncertain of the welcome he would receive. Beatrice started waving to him, grinning.

"Hey, look who's here," Ollie said, appearing as happy to see Xan as Beatrice was.

A group of people moved in front of Xan, blocking their view. All of a sudden, the music and singing stopped. There was an instant of absolute silence, and then the restaurant began to buzz with excited but hushed voices.

Beatrice glanced around the room, not understanding what was happening. She had thought the village witches would greet Xan warmly and be eager to make amends. But no one was moving forward to welcome him. In fact, everyone seemed to be rooted in place. This was all very strange.

Beatrice stood up, intending to bring Xan back to their table. She caught sight of him again through the crowd, still standing beside the door, and then she realized that he wasn't alone. A head moved so that Beatrice had a clear view—and she froze in astonishment. She never would have imagined this, but she could see it for herself: Xan had brought Nina Bailey to Friar's Lantern.

Beatrice forgot about the people with their heads together whispering, and started pushing through the crowd toward her mother. When Mrs. Bailey saw Beatrice, she burst into tears. The next instant, Beatrice reached her mother and they hugged each other.

"I'm so glad you're here," Beatrice said, crying now herself.

"Your friend Xan said I had to come," Mrs. Bailey said, wiping furiously at the tears that streamed down her face. "He said I should be here to celebrate with you. I'm so proud of you!" she said fiercely, and held Beatrice tighter.

Beatrice looked over her mother's shoulder at Xan. He was smiling.

"Thank you," Beatrice whispered.

Xan nodded, his smile spreading wider.

"I should have told you," Mrs. Bailey was saying. "I always meant to, but I was so ashamed."

"It doesn't matter now," Beatrice replied.

Then all of a sudden it seemed that everyone was crowding around them, jostling Beatrice as they reached out to her mother.

"It's good you could be here with Beatrice."

"I've thought about you often, Nina."

"That daughter of yours—she's Dally Rumpe's worst nightmare. We're sure proud of her."

"We've missed you, Nina Merriwether. Glad you're back."

Beatrice disengaged herself from the tangle of bodies, and stepped back to catch her breath. She saw Teddy,

Ollie, and Cyrus standing nearby and went over to join them.

"Wow," Ollie said, grinning. "Some surprise, huh?"

"I'll say," Beatrice agreed.

Then Laurel handed her a dainty linen handkerchief, and Beatrice dabbed at her wet face.

"I never thought I'd see this day," Laurel said, eyes spilling over as she reached into her pocket for another hanky. Then she noticed Xan standing nearby, and she said, "Get over here, you old smuggler you."

Beatrice was surprised to see Xan comply without protest, and even more surprised when Laurel threw her arms around Xan and gave him a huge hug.

Before long, everybody seemed to be hugging everybody else, and many were turning weepy, as well.

"Isn't this the best day?" Primrose said to Beatrice, then blew her nose with a satisfied honk. She looked as if she couldn't decide whether to laugh or cry. "I guess you won't be staying with us after all," she said finally.

"Not this time," Beatrice said. "But I'm really going to miss you."

"You'll be back," Primrose said stoutly. "And no matter where you go, you've earned the right to call yourself a witch of Friar's Lantern."

Beatrice was watching as Aura Featherstone and Skye Drummond approached her mother together. When Nina Bailey saw them, she stood riveted, a look of uncertainty on her face. Then Skye reached out her hand and the tension seemed to melt away.

About that time, Thaddeus Thigpin was elbowing his way toward Dr. Featherstone.

"What is the meaning of this?" the director demanded, giving Nina Bailey full benefit of his scowl. "That witch has been banished from the Sphere. She has no right to be here!"

Expecting Dr. Featherstone to reply in her usual soothing and tactful way, Beatrice was taken aback when the auburn-haired witch said curtly, "Get over it, Thaddeus. She won't be here long, and Beatrice deserves to share this moment with her mother."

Dr. Thigpin gave Aura Featherstone a startled look that quickly deteriorated to a glare. Then he turned on his heel and headed for Puddifoot, who had just appeared with another tray of drinks.

Laurel brought plates of sandwiches for Nina Bailey and Xan, and someone else gave them glasses of witches brew. Then Magnus began playing his tin whistle and people started singing again. Beatrice noticed quite a few witches coming over to have a word with Xan and then slapping him on the back before they moved on.

"It's ended rather well," Beatrice said with satisfaction. "Better than I ever could have imagined."

"It has," Teddy agreed. Then she frowned, as if something critical had just occurred to her. "Do you think someone's made an official note about me going into Werewolf Close with you and targeting the werewolves? I'd hate for the committee to overlook it."

Beatrice smiled. "I wouldn't worry, Teddy. I expect it's all been recorded by now in *The Bailiwick Family History*."

The only imperfect thing about the evening was that it passed too quickly. In what seemed like a very short time, Xan was telling Beatrice that he should be taking her mother home.

"I'll come with you," Beatrice said quickly.

"We'll all come," Ollie said.

When everyone realized that Beatrice and her mother were leaving, they gathered around to say their farewells, and then followed them out into Cattail Court.

Laurel reached up to adjust the brim on Beatrice's hat. "Don't forget now," she said, her eyes glistening in the light from Xan's lantern, "we'll always have a room ready for you. I don't want to wait another twelve years to see you. You'll need a new hat before then."

"It's all been discussed," Primrose said gruffly, and winked at Beatrice. "She'll be back before you know it."

Beatrice blew her bangs aside and looked at the many dear faces around her. There were Dr. Featherstone and Dr. Meadowmouse, Peregrine and Longshank, and all the witches of Friar's Lantern.

Beatrice felt her eyes mist over. She turned quickly to follow her mother and her friends across the courtyard, with Cayenne perched on her shoulder. Beatrice looked back once and gave a final wave before disappearing under the arch.

As they walked down Will-o'-the-wisp Road, Beatrice realized that she was tired. The events of the past twenty-four hours were finally catching up with her. The others must have felt the same way because no one spoke, even after they had reached the wharf.

While she waited for Teddy to climb into Xan's boat, Beatrice stood on the pier and took one last look across the river. That's when she saw them. A half dozen pale bluish lights moved slowly through the swamp.

Beatrice blinked. She didn't understand this at all. Innes wouldn't be sending out anyone with lanterns until next week. So if not Innes, and not Xan, and not Dally Rumpe—*who?*

Suddenly a smile flashed across Beatrice's face as she realized that it didn't matter *who* or *what*. The witches of Friar's Lantern had the magic and the mystery of their lights. And something told Beatrice that they always would.